The Way of the Odin Brotherhood

To Ari who forged the dream,
and Max, who showed me the way

The Way of the Odin Brotherhood

by Jack Wolf

Published by
Mandrake of Oxford
PO Box 250
OXFORD
OX1 1AP (UK)

A CIP catalogue record for this book is available from the British Library and the US Library of Congress.

Contents

Foreword

"I have sometimes wondered if it were possible that unrecognized forces of the past or present—or even the future— work through the thoughts and actions of living men."
- Robert E. Howard,   December 14, 1933

Mysteries have always intrigued me. For example, Vallalar, also known as Ramalinga Adigal, disappeared from his one-room residence in Mettukuppam, India on January 30, 1874. After he had given his last and most famous lecture on the "nature of the powers that lie beyond us and move us," he locked himself into his home and told his followers *never* to open the door. He said anyone entering would find nothing.

Vallalar's seclusion generated rumors, and the British Government finally forced the door in May. They found an empty room and no clues. The facts were reported in the *Madras District Gazetteer.*

* * *

In my own life I have experienced the enigma of the Odin Brotherhood. This secret society, composed of men and women who use darkness and stealth to preserve the lore of old gods and the purity of old ways, thrives on mystery.

Who are they? Why are they here? Why does legend surround their origin?

No one really knows the answers to such questions, but it is clear that anyone who encounters the Brotherhood is changed. Life has many moments of transformation—as an elderly Ethiopian woman once said to Leo Viktor Frobenius (1873 – 1938), the fabled scholar, when a woman is deflowered, or when a pubescent boy undergoes the ordeal of circumcision, each is changed forever—but when men and women encounter the Odin Brotherhood, they are transfigured.

Since publishing my little work on the Odin Brotherhood—in 1992—my contacts with the arcane have increased in number. I have been contacted by an alleged time traveler, I have been visited by a woman claiming to be from Odin, I have received cryptic verses (postmarked from Frankfurt, Germany) supposedly written by Odin himself, I have been offered membership in a French suicide cult, I have been asked to help with an exorcism of an adolescent deaf girl, and I have been visited by a traumatized woman who claimed to be a refugee from a subterranean world where humans are "bred like cattle and hunted like rabbits." The list is extensive.

My hope was to be invited to join the Academy of Secrets, founded by Giambattista della Porta (1535? – 1615) and open only to those who had made important discoveries, but that has not yet happened.

Are any or all of these contacts connected to the Odin Brotherhood? As a believer in the process that Professor Carl Jung called "synchronicity," or "meaningful coincidences," I think that they are.

I cannot prove the linkage, but I do know that by publishing my slender book I did meet Jack Wolf. A Canadian, an acolyte of E. Max Hyatt, an associate of respected *seiðr*-woman named Cassandra Strong, Jack Wolf is the man who crafted the volume that you now hold.

And now, as my life has changed, so shall his.

* * *

After remaining hidden for so long, why is information on the

Odin Brotherhood now emerging? Members still keep their involvement secret, but why is their "ancient lore" now appearing in books, articles, videos, and Internet sites?

Perhaps, as our civilization dies, we are being offered a "beacon of light."

Many historians date the decline of the West from World War I, and is it a coincidence that weeks before the war, on July 20, 1914, that modern humans rediscovered *Trois-Frères?*

Used for 20,000 years as a religious site, this huge labyrinth, reached in total darkness via a narrow passage—only one foot high and 120 feet long—was dedicated to the old gods of Europe, when man hunted savage beasts, dressed in rawhide, and huddled around open fires.

Perhaps, in this time of distress, the old gods and goddesses from the era of the "Ice" are stirring once more.

And, they are using Jack Wolf to help us.

Mark Mirabello, Ph.D
Professor of History
Shawnee State University
May, 2012

JACK WOLF

Acknowledgements

The quest to learn the Way of the Odin Brotherhood has been a long one. Its origins came many years ago, when I was a young man searching for the truth of my pagan roots. I delved deeply into my ancestral past, I studied and I journeyed, ever seeking what I thought of as the 'core' idea of my tribal origins.

Along the way I was very fortunate to have some great teachers; men and women who, it would seem, appeared on the road of my destiny at precisely the time when I needed their guidance. To this end I would like to thank the following people for their help, assistance and encouragement over the years.

Oliver Moon, who was there from the beginning and taught me there was always more to be learned just over the horizon.

Ari Torinsson, who helped me discover the trail back to my Northern roots and showed me the deeper ways of the Warrior and the sharp edge of spirit.

E. Max Hyatt, a friend, mentor and a person of deep knowledge and spiritual conviction. Max was the first to offer me clues to the path to the Odin Brotherhood. An ever-discerning seeker of knowledge, Max was convinced the Odin Brotherhood was a legitimate secret society and what they had to teach was important to the world. This great man and respected Gothi encouraged me to delve deeper and learn what I could.

Wolfgang Schmidt, a sea captain and old-time pagan from Germany who showed me the Old Ways are to be lived and not simply studied.

Werner von Otto, a dear friend and a man of Njord who taught that ritual was merely a means to an end and never an end in itself.

Tom Joy, who was instrumental in teaching me about the Northern Folkway, a unique worldview of the Old Ways and a trail that led me closer to the Odin Brotherhood. Tom is very close to the Old Ways and lives them every day. He has long been a deep inspiration to me.

Dr. Mark Mirabello of Shawnee State University was of particular help when it came to discovering the deeper keys of this hidden society and the study of secret societies in general. Indeed, it was he who set me on the path that would ultimately result in my eventual contact with the cryptic Odin Brotherhood themselves. Though his knowledge of the Odin Brotherhood has stemmed from purely academic and historical interest he has, as one would expect of a professor, done his research very thoroughly.

Cassandra Wolf, without whose encouragement, editing abilities, and critical reviews of my work this book in its present form would never have become reality.

And of course my appreciation also goes out to the enigmatic and anonymous members of the Odin Brotherhood themselves who, through various means and channels, have kindly communicated with me and answered many of my questions. Their words have provided a very valuable resource in the writing of this book.

And last but certainly not least: Thanks are due to a friend I know only by his single name, Crow. His deep knowledge of the ways of the Odin Brotherhood filled in so many gaps in my own knowledge that without his assistance this book would likely be much less interesting than I hope it is.

A note on citations and sources:

When I began work on this book I spent considerable time pondering how I might provide citations for the work. However, as the majority of material here has been provided via oral tradition and teachings and also from anonymous sources, this has proven difficult. Thus I have indicated specific sources only where this has been possible.

I would like to note also that the opinions of my sources are indeed their own and do not necessarily represent my own thoughts unless I have indicated that in the text.

JACK WOLF

Introduction

The Black Spiral Prophecy: The beginning of my journey

It was nearly twenty-five years ago my journey to the Odin Brotherhood began.

Naturally I had absolutely no idea anything like the Odin Brotherhood existed back then, and even if I had it is likely I would only have been mildly interested. It is said that for all things there is a season, and I was probably not ready for such knowledge at that time.

I was a young man then, back in 1986, and like many my age I was still attempting to find myself; to discover exactly who I was and what my purpose was.

I felt the deep call of my pagan ancestors from the ancient European past, yet there was so much going on around me I at first had difficulty grasping those roots. It was a tumultuous time, made even more so by the fact that my grandfather, a man who had taught me much and influenced me greatly, had passed on only the year before.

I was drifting spiritually, lost and feeling more lost each day. I felt as though I had lost so much with the passing of my grandfather and these feelings were made all the more intense as they were fuelled by the passions which may be found in the fiery hearts of only the young.

Luckily for me, and I have seemed always to be fortunate in such things, I was taken under the wing of one of my grandfather's best friends. I had met this man several years before in the company of my grandfather and had occasionally had some good conversations with him. My grandfather trusted him implicitly and one could tell simply by watching the two men that they were as brothers.

My grandfather had pointed out to me on many occasions that

his friend was a good one to show me the deeper parts of my northern heritage; that he had much to teach.

Thus, my grandfather's friend, a hale companion of many years, became another of my teachers. He was large, blonde-haired and ice-blue-eyed with the almost stereotypical look of a fierce Norseman. His name was Ari.

He was the first person I had ever met other than my grandfather who had truly walked the ways of my ancestors and Ari knew well the ways of my northern European ancestors. Before him I had no idea any of those old traditions had survived other than as fragmentary, borrowed practices in use by various neo-pagan groups. Before him, I had thought those old ways and the people who walked with those old Gods had long since faded into the past.

Ari was living proof that it was not so, and as I began to learn from him I came to the realization that he was not the only one of his kind; that indeed there were many more like him about in the world – though still a tiny fragment of the population, there *were* more.

And so, as time went on, I learned much about the Old Ways from my grandfather's friend. Indeed Ari was a Master of a semi-hidden pagan tradition himself and he had massive amounts to teach – and perhaps I will cover that in another book.

He taught me of the Gods and the Goddesses (or the **Elder-Kin** as he often termed them); of the sagas and the ancient tales from long ago. He was a grand storyteller and in his words a person could literally *see* the vistas of the ancient world opening up.

I remember feeling deep warmth flowing from within me as I listened to the stories. I felt the rising excitement that came with each tale. I laughed at the caperings of trickster Loki; I felt the surge of victory in the exploits of Thor and I felt the hushed awe that one feels when they hear tell of Odin.

To the great ladies of the Vanir and the Aesir I felt connected as well; I felt delight in the stories of the lovely, innocent Idunna in her garden, and a strange attraction-yet-wariness as I was told about the Goddess Freyja.

Ari did not mince words. He was a master in the telling of tales yet he was also very direct in his discussions about the *true* nature of these Old Ones. He emphasized that these were not the Gods of the weak, but the Elder Kin of those with the Bloodfire in their veins. He made a point of telling me even the mellowest appearing of these Old Ones had a very sharp edge; that one had to be bold, yet wary in dealing with them – for they were all eons-sharpened instruments of fate.

Ari told me once, 'Even the lovely and compassionate Idunna, or the wise and matronly grandmother Frigga would tear your head off without the slightest hesitation - in an instant - if you were to cross her the wrong way.'

He always spoke of the Gods and Goddesses, of the Vaettir, of the wights, the spirits of the land, in real time. They were NOW. To him they were not myths, not simply old stories told by Elders around a fire. They were very viscerally real.

'The Gods and Goddesses walk with us, right now – in this world,' he used to say. 'They are not something of the past. They come here to our little island universe to visit us because we are their kin.'

I recall once, very clearly as if it was yesterday, Ari leaning forward toward me over the fire, his eyes bright with the yellow-gold dance of the flames between us, the shadows dancing upon his craggy bearded face.

'Never make the mistake of thinking these are not real beings. I have seen them. They are quite real.'

I was captivated. The hunger within me grew and I wanted more. It seemed my appetite was insatiable, yet each time I asked him for a tale Ari had yet one more 'on the back burner' as he used to say.

He also taught me as with any great thing simplicity was the key to success. While he showed me his simple rites, his ways of honoring the Old Ones, he continually emphasized the fact that even the best rituals and tools are ultimately only crutches – eventually abandoned by the strong who had learned well what was needed, but yet clutched closely in perpetuation by the weak.

He taught that these Elder Kin, these Gods and Goddesses of the north, did not appreciate complex 'carryings on' as he used to put it, but rather simple, direct means of communication.

'As soon as someone starts feeling the need to get involved with complicated rituals,' he once told me, 'they are not moving forward but rather they are reverting. They are building a better crutch. They are probably trying to revert back to the Christian programming they had as a kid and they don't even realize it.'

His way was a simple one. He lived in deep harmony with the spirits of the land, honored his ancestors and even had peaceful relations with the ghosts of the wood near his home. He spoke with the Gods directly and in a simple, almost casual fashion, much in the same way as I had learned to approach the Aboriginal Elders I had known; with respect and in the fashion those of much greater wisdom and experience deserve to be treated.

And one of the gifts of time and experience for Ari was the talent for deep and intense prophetic dreams he often had. He told me that ever since he had been a boy he had experienced powerful visions. Often they were simply ways by which the Otherworld was helping him to learn more about things, but other times these dreams were telling him of things to come. His interpretation of them was seldom off by much.

And one of these – the one that originally set me on the journey to discover more about the Odin Brotherhood, was the vision I came to know as the Black Spiral prophecy.

One night as I sat with Ari in his modest home, he told me about a vision he had experienced. He told me this because we had been discussing my future and I had told him that I was quite unsure as to what I should be doing with my life. I had told him I wanted to honor my ancestry but I wanted to do so in a way that did not seem like some kind of half-measure. It had been bothering me a lot and I had come to him for guidance on the subject.

Ari told me he strongly believed that a part of my destiny was to teach and to write about what I had learned. He believed that I had a destiny in something he called the '*re-awakening*'; a process in which more and more people would begin to discover their ancient pagan roots and that slowly through this action, millennia of damage caused by the attempted cultural genocide against the Old Ways would begin to be repaired.

He told me the coming decades would be important times not only for our people, our pagan heritage, but also for the very species itself. He believed the reawakening was a part of a larger, human-species awakening he hoped would occur in time to prevent the ideologies of those he called the 'World-killers' from annihilating the entire planet and everything on it.

He told me nature herself has ways of dealing with disease and indeed, the ideologies which had been responsible for the raping of minds, bodies, and souls – and the very life of our sacred planet – were seen as sickly wasting disease by the Elder Kin themselves.

'Nature has a way of dealing with disease,' he said, 'and one of those ways, just like in an animal's body, is the creation of antibodies, like those hunter-killer cells that attack a virus.'

He believed the reawakening was a part of that process; that as human kind began to awaken from millennia of disease-induced slave behavior it would also begin to move forward in ways that could save the world.

One aspect of the reawakening was for long-hidden secrets to be revealed. I was told the genocide which was attempted on pagan thought and culture was never completed; that fragments remained and those which remained survived by moving deeper into what he termed the 'Hidden Glades'; places where the thing he termed the

LIE could never reach them. Such fragments of truth often took the form of hidden traditions or even secret societies.

These groups, Ari told me, were like tiny lifeboats carrying time capsules of knowledge and lore that had escaped destruction over thousands of years – and like little seeds, once planted they would have the chance to grow great and strong once again – like the mighty ash, Yggdrasil, or the mighty oak grandfathers of the ancient groves.

Ari told me of his vision. He told me that even though it had come to him years before I was born, he believed in some way it related to me, that I would have a hand in the process.

The vision had come to him in the autumn of 1957 as he visited the ruins of an ancient Native Indian longhouse on the Pacific coast. As he had camped in the area for several days, Ari told me that he had experienced some of the most profound dreams and visions of his life.

Here is a portion of what he wrote down concerning the experience: '...and I saw in this dream that I was standing in the center of a grove of ancient trees. It was autumn and colored leaves were blowing everywhere on the wind. I looked down and I saw a piece of flat stone near my feet, barely pushing up above the ground.

As I watched, the stone grew in size, breaking free of the soil and rising before me until a dark menhir, some ten feet high, stood at the center of the grove.

Suddenly it was as though I was above it; a raven on the wind and I could see that the dark menhir was but one of a band of brother-stones spread across the world in an immense, ancient spiral. Each Brother-stone represented a clan of sacred warriors who would come into being to protect the Lore and the sacred places in the world from the coming storm.'

'And these brotherhoods, these gatherings of the lore are out there right now,' he told me, a barely suppressed urgency in his voice. 'Most of these are probably hidden, seeking to protect the traditions they hold,' he said. 'It will be important for you to look out for them, especially the ones that have preserved fragments of the lore of the north.'

And thus was the seed planted in my mind. Thus was the idea that such groups of people were out there instilled in my soul. It became a kind of quest for me and I set out to search for them. Though my journey took me to many places over the years it eventually led me to a knowledge of the Odin Brotherhood.

* * *

Years passed and over time I began to see more and more that the world was filled with signs and symbols that were there for anyone to see; one simply had to know where to look and to be mindful as to what it was they were looking for – and yet often such signs can appear when one least expects to see them.

Some years later, while working on a video production deep in the city I found myself in a particularly dark and dismal section of what we here in Vancouver call the Downtown Eastside. This area, once the fashionable center of town a hundred years back, has been lost to poverty and strife over the decades until now it is the home of many of the poor and disenfranchised. Boarded-up storefronts, trash-strewn laneways roamed by the homeless, drug dealers and gangsters alike make this area of town a grim and dangerous place.

It was, however, considered to be an appropriate locale to shoot the video we were working on and thus, one rainy evening, I found myself, along with a few others, running power cables into a darkened underground warren so set lighting could be accommodated.

I worked my way along a basement hallway, cluttered with the detritus of extended (and not too sanitary) human habitation, and as we plugged in a set of work lights I was rather startled to note that amongst the other, more generic graffiti splashed on the red brick wall there were several neatly placed runic scripts ending in a bind-rune at the end of the passage. These were not randomly scrawled 'tags' left by someone marking territory, but seemed to be something deeper; more magical. I could sense the intent of the person who had placed them there.

My co-worker realized we were short a few cables and returned outside to retrieve them, leaving me momentarily alone with the mysterious markings.

The second thing that surprised me was the presence of the old man standing in an old, worn-out black trench coat in a corner only a few feet away. It had been nearly pitch black down there yet there he was, perfectly comfortable in the darkness. He smiled kindly at my sudden start and asked me what we were doing down there. I told him about our project and he smiled. He told me that this place where we were working would be relatively safe compared to some of the other areas around.

I reassured him that later there would be security while we were filming. He smiled again and pointed to a place on the wall where there was a simple eye-shaped glyph spray-painted in blue on the old bricks.

'The eye of Odin,' he said simply.

I was again, quite surprised. Such a place was the last location I had expected to find folk who honored the Old Ways.

'He comes around here sometimes,' the old fellow said with a glint in his eye as though he was imparting a special secret. 'People have seen him even though most people didn't know who he really was. Sometimes he helps and sometimes he just...watches.'

'Who?' I asked rather incredulously. 'Odin?'

I looked at the man. He looked back at me. He knew something and that something was that although he and I were seemingly from different worlds the one thing we shared in common was the connection to the Old Ways. Somehow he *knew* I too walked the ways of the ancestors in the same fashion of the heart he himself did. There was no malice in him, no trickery - just a simple truth; a knowing.

'Odin never left us,' the old man said, sensing my hesitation.

'Christians and other types would tell us the Old Ones were fairy stories or myths or even evil, but there are many of us who know different, even out here in the streets.'

After a moment he added, 'Times are changing, son. Odin's people are finally waking up. The Brotherhood of Odin is everywhere.'

He then told me he had better get moving along. He asked me rather hesitantly if I might be able to spare him a couple of bucks for food. I was glad to oblige. I gave him the few dollars I had in my pocket at the time. It seemed the least I could do, considering the revelation he had just imparted to me.

The mysterious old man thanked me, shook my hand with a firm grip, wished me luck in my venture and, with a grin, made his way down the hall, up the stairs and into the rainy night. I realized then how foolish I had been in being surprised at finding evidence of Odin's folk down there – in the depths of poverty and despair. I realized that indeed, the Gods would be where their people were, no matter where that was...

That night in the basement of the rundown old building left an indelible impression on me. I never forgot the feeling I had experienced when in the sudden flash of the work-light I had realized the wall before me had been covered in runes. I had seen too that my co-worker had noticed not a thing; he had simply seen the markings as another sort of graffiti and dismissed it from his mind.

He was not one of 'us'; he had not seen the markings for what they were.

'Times are changing, son. Odin's people are finally waking up.'

'The Brotherhood of Odin is everywhere.'

The signs and symbols of this are all around us.

* * *

I am not a member of the Odin Brotherhood, but rather could be considered an interested student of its traditions. Whether I might, some day in the future, ever become a member of the Brotherhood remains to be seen, yet that is not really the subject of this book.

Instead, I would like to share the story of the journey that led me to explore this mysterious order, and indeed to share the knowledge of it I have gained along the way. Ari's vision and teachings were the beginning but the road in between those early days and now, as I write, has been a lengthy and sometimes perilous one.

The Odin Brotherhood, its very existence unknown to the world outside its own circles for nearly six centuries, has emerged slightly from the shadows only very recently, most notably through the writings of Dr. Mark Mirabello. There are reasons for this: changes in the world and prophecies have urged the revelation of elder knowledge, knowledge that in some instances has been retained only by the lore-keepers of the Odin Brotherhood. It is the quest for such knowledge that has drawn me along the trail of the years and it has culminated in the pages you see before you.

Over the past few years in particular I have opened a dialogue with initiated members of the Odin Brotherhood itself. As the Odin Brotherhood is a true secret society, managing an actual means of communication with its enigmatic members was no simple task. It took a considerable effort and a certain degree of trust, yet eventually the work paid off.

I now have several valuable connections, there are some individuals, actual members of the Brotherhood, who have, when it pleased them, consented to advise me from time to time. I have also been helped by a notable historian in the writing of this book.

Finally, I have the honor of knowing a fellow who has walked the path of what he calls *the deeper Odinism*. He is a person of considerable knowledge of the Odin Brotherhood and a warrior of deep pagan commitments. Like myself he has journeyed far and he has been kind enough to share what he knows with me. Indeed, he plans to initiate into the Brotherhood soon. He has shared much of his journey with me. What will become of our relationship after that, I cannot say.

I have learnt immeasurably from these connections and through studies of my own, though I have little doubt that what I know now is just the tip of the iceberg. I am, after all, an outsider and not privy to the deeper workings of this shadowy tradition.

As to the members of the Brotherhood with whom I have been in communication they are obviously quite aware of my existence and indeed of my quest concerning their tradition. Much to my surprise they have actually encouraged me to some extent, telling me that while the identities of their membership must forever remain a secret, the lore itself is priceless and should be made available to all who would seek it.

Thus, here for those who would know, is the story of my exploration of the long hidden bastion of the Odin Brotherhood.

I

Hearthside: On the Trail of the Odin Brotherhood

I sat quietly in the darkened room, bathed only in the flickering glow of candles I had set upon the living room table in front of me. The house was enveloped in the cold calm of the Hour of the Wolf; that time between the midnight hour and the harbingers of dawn's light. I could hear the wind picking up outside and knew there was a storm on the way.

A wine glass full of golden mead, set on the wooden table, sparkled in the light of the candles, beckoning me. I gave in and took a small sip, savoring the flavor of captured summer, and then sat back in the seat. I was exhausted. I had just finished a lengthy conversation with a mentor of mine, Odinist, respected scholar and Elder, Max.

Max and I had experienced many such conversations before, often pertaining to the history and lore of Old Europe or the deep nature of pagan tribalism. Each time I had considered myself privileged to be the recipient of my friend's time-seasoned wisdom; each time I received a bounty of fresh knowledge that did nothing but propel my mind and heart ever forward on my quest for understanding.

But this night had been somewhat different. It had, just like many times before, been the source of deep enlightenment, but this time the subject of our talk had been running on a slightly different trail; that of the enigmatic Odin Brotherhood. The discussion had carried a kind of intensity that colored it in a way I had not experienced before with Max. In the end it had me filled with a renewed fiery curiosity and a form of mental exhaustion at the same time.

I had heard only misty, half remembered rumors before this time, bits and pieces of stories and repeated rumors coming from pagan and heathen friends I knew. In almost every case the things I had heard were fragmentary at best and followed by the declaration that the whole thing was made up; an internet hoax or a sociological study of some sort...along with comments like, 'But wouldn't it be cool if something like this really existed?'

As I had long been interested in secret societies I put a bit of time into trying to learn more but had not dug up much information. Like many projects I had rolling around in my mind and inside my file cabinet I had set it aside for further investigation at perhaps a later date.

It was a fading memory when Max suddenly brought it up that evening. The abruptness with which he had done so had momentarily startled me.

'What are your thoughts on the Odin Brotherhood?' had been the question.

We had been discussing the nature of orthodoxy in Odinism and how Max, as other teachers I had learned from in my time agreed, held concerns that too many modern pagan organizations were falling victim to a kind of *creeping orthodoxy*. That is, many had not completely divorced themselves from the childhood programming they had received — usually in Christian or Judaic doctrines — and subconsciously it was sneaking back into the methodologies of many modern pagan groups.

I recall thinking about how well Max and my old mentor Ari would have gotten along as they shared many of the same viewpoints on the world.

And suddenly, as though going into a high speed turn on a foggy cliff-side road, Max changed direction.

'What are your thoughts on the Odin Brotherhood?'

The question threw me off balance. My friend was a very direct man and passionate in his way but usually he stuck to the point and did not venture off on tangents so much as many others I knew were accustomed to doing. I had not brought up the subject with him before, even when I was keen about the stories I had heard, mainly because I considered Max to be old school. That is, a very up-front, to the point, lore-based/history-based Odinist who did not have time for what he might consider to be New Age rumors, conspiracy theories or internet hoaxes. Thus, out of respect, I had not spoken with him about it.

Next I wondered if his sudden question was some kind of a test to determine my seriousness in studying the Old Ways...or perhaps even a rough joke.

So I told him what I knew: that the Odin Brotherhood was supposed to be a mysterious secret society which held hidden lore and that its membership was secret. I also told him I had heard this organization claimed to be centuries old, maybe five hundred years or more.

Max asked me what I actually thought about that. He wanted to know whether I believed it or not.

'I would very much like to,' I replied. 'But I am still not sure about it.'

With all of the garbage floating around on the internet and elsewhere it is often difficult to make a clear determination about some things.

Max then told me that he had read a very interesting book written by a historian named Mark Mirabello who taught at a 'university out east.' Max went on at length about the impact Dr. Mirabello's book had had on him; how at a very deep instinctive level he somehow knew that the author was not playing games – that he was trying to convey a highly controversial package of knowledge in a world that might 'burn him for it.'

Max told me how he was so entranced by the work he read it aloud to his family in the evenings, and how they sat there, intensely intrigued with the possibilities that this book suggested.

I had heard that there was a book out there called the *Odin Brotherhood*, but I had never gotten around to ordering a copy. Now, both curious and extremely motivated, I told Max that at first I had imagined he was either messing with me or trying to figure out how serious I was in walking the ways of the Elder Kin. I had experienced these kinds of tests with other teachers and I knew it was well within their rights to do such thing; to make such determinations of those whom they instructed.

He told me he was not kidding around; he was dead serious. Then he asked me a question that sparked my curiosity about Dr. Mirabello's book even more.

'How did you feel when you first read the Hávamál?'

I jokingly responded that it would depend on which translation of said tome, and his response was 'Whatever one you like best.'

There are numerous translations of this work, a segment of the Poetic Edda, some easier to relate to than the others. My favorite was that translated by W.H. Auden & P.B. Taylor.

I thought about Max's question for a little while. The Hávamál is a deeply inspiring work and it gives us a powerful impression on life as seen through the eyes and wisdom of Odin. Indeed the very word Hávamál is an old word meaning *Words of the High*, or the words of Odin.

I recall sitting there the first evening I had obtained a copy and devouring the entire thing in a night, then re-reading its verses more slowly and deliberately. I recall the realizations which came with the knowledge that each verse held so much more insight than the one before it: wisdom that seemed to grow more profound as one probed deeper into its meaning.

I told Max this and his response was something like, 'Well, Mirabello's book is not the Hávamál, but it will inspire you to wake up much like the Book of Har does. I suggest strongly that you get a copy and read it and then let me know what you think.'

And I took my friend's advice and sought out a copy. Max was right: it was certainly not the Hávamál, but it was intriguing and enticing in a similar manner. Written in the form of an interview between Professor Mirabello and a member (or possibly multiple members) of the mysterious Brotherhood, the book describes the history and culture of a pagan society dedicated to the lore of the Norse Gods and Goddesses; a society long hidden in the midst of the world in order to protect itself and its treasures of knowledge from annihilation.

It is not a particularly lengthy work, but a fascinating one. It drew me in from the very first page and before I knew it I was finished and desperately craving more. I understood what Max was saying about this book, and like my friend, it had me thinking *'These people sound very much like myself in their worldview.'*

It was not long after this I began searching for more information on the Odin Brotherhood. There was, naturally, very little available in the libraries and even though the internet had begun its exponential expansion in the world I could find little regarding the enigmatic Brotherhood other than references back to Dr. Mirabello's book or to the various conspiracy theory websites which were beginning to abound in cyberspace. I reported my frustration to Max after a couple of weeks of this and he told me that he too had had little success in learning more about the Brotherhood than what he had gleaned from Dr. Mirabello's book. Max suggested I try to look 'somewhere off the beaten track' and even perhaps to contact the author of the Odin Brotherhood book himself.

I took Max's advice and began to put out subtle inquiries within the pagan and heathen/Odinist communities with the hope I might come across someone who knew something more than had been reported in the book. Working from my knowledge and experience as an undergraduate student at the University of British Columbia, I knew professors were impossibly busy people and so I put off bothering Dr. Mirabello for the time being. I hoped I would be able to fill in a few of the blanks myself before I went to the man who was considered an authority – or at least a conveyor of information about the Brotherhood.

The responses I got back from my connections in the various pagan communities were not overly promising. They ranged from blunt disbelief in the existence of the Odin Brotherhood; that it was either a prank, a rumor or a sociological experiment of some kind, to wary suggestions that such a thing might have existed but no longer did.

In this early phase of my search I turned up little that was promising. It was what I expected, because if the Odin Brotherhood actually existed and they were indeed a true secret society, what would be the point of having reams of information available if the whole idea was that they were 'a secret' in the first place?

I brought this back to my friend and he told me the best route would be to go directly to the source – or at least to one who had been close to the source. I had a feeling that at this point Max had access to sources of information he was not ready to speak about, but I did not want to press him on it. I left it at that for the time being.

And time passed. Day to day life got in the way of the quest and I found myself side tracked onto what seemed like a hundred different side trails.

A wise man once told me that one should be very cautious about how he uses time for once it has slipped through your fingers it is truly lost to you. These were wise words and words I wish I had considered more deeply. How much time we waste in things that are thoroughly mundane and have little or no bearing upon the truly important things in life?

As with many of the projects I found myself engaged in over time I left the Odin Brotherhood project to one side while I dealt with the myriad of other things we modern humans play at, not giving proper thought to the passing of time.

And it was during this space between the acts of life my friend and mentor, Max, passed from this world, gone to be with Odin in his halls at last. Max had not been in the greatest health during his final years and in the end a sudden downturn took this great and learned man to the realm of the Gods.

It shocked me out of my inactivity and when I was finished with a period of mourning for a great teacher, I set my feet back on the path he and I had shared in the end; the quest to discover more about the Odin Brotherhood.

I at last made contact with Dr. Mirabello, initially to pass on to him the news that Max had passed, and was pleased to discover he and Max were acquainted. Following that initial contact I found though he was naturally a very busy man, Dr. Mirabello was very gracious with his time and indeed was very open to sharing his experiences and knowledge with me.

It was at this point that my focus on the Odin Brotherhood began in earnest.

As I have mentioned already, much of what is known to the world in general pertaining to the Odin Brotherhood comes to us by way of Dr. Mirabello's book. There are tales circulating around that there are other works about; that there are hidden volumes and other sources of information out there available to those who are skilled or lucky enough to discover them. However, to his knowledge, Dr. Mirabello has told me he has not seen any of them himself. He did have a few research suggestions and following these and other such pointers, I set out to make some more connections.

One of the best pieces of advice I received with regard to making connections came originally from a close friend of mine. I spent several months doing all I could to track down any trace that might lead me to the Odin Brotherhood, yet all I managed to do was uncover tiny scraps and rumors for the most part. I felt I was at a dead end. I informed my friend of this and he had a suggestion: that since making contact with folk who are cautious about revealing themselves will be difficult to do – the best thing to do was to attract their notice and hope they might come to you.

I had considered this kind of approach before and had pursued it only minimally, yet with my friend's suggestion I went at it again. I began making queries in as many places as I could, especially on the internet where I suspected there might be at least a few actual members of the secret order. I increased my participation on pagan, heathen and Odinist web-forums and generally let it be known I was respectfully interested in learning more. I even tried the Dr. Mirabello route and began frequenting more and more bookstores in the hope I might inadvertently come across an 'agent' of the mysterious brotherhood.

Well, I certainly did not encounter any enigmatic persons in the shadowy aisles of the bookstores, nor in the depths of the library stacks...nor did I expect any immediate response to my new courses of inquiry. In fact, I wasn't sure if I would receive any legitimate responses at all, though I was certainly not surprised when more than a few people contacted me looking to learn what I had learned about the Brotherhood. Naturally there was also an assortment of jokers and outright liars who made all kinds of silly claims.

The Odin Brotherhood has a saying: '***The unworthy exclude themselves.***' I found that to be a most enlightening piece of wisdom and indeed it helped me filter out the crazies from the more earnest contacts I made. Yet none of the early 'connections' were the real deal in my thinking; not one of them was that authentic, electric personal contact I had been hoping for.

I had done my best to help others who, like myself were seeking to know more, and I continued to make queries and to participate on forums, yet I felt perhaps what I had to offer was not of sufficient interest to stir the Brotherhood from their comfortable secret silence.

Months passed and life went on.

And then, finally, as I had begun to lighten up on the queries, to back away from the intensity of the forums; as life began to fall back into normal patterns, I received an enigmatic looking e-mail that simply said: 'Would you know more?'

I was immediately inclined to dismiss the message as a hoax or perhaps the work of yet another ego-driven crazy person out there. Yet I recalled the conversation with that old man in the rank downtown cellar when he said: '*Times are changing, son. Odin's people are finally waking up. The Brotherhood of Odin is everywhere.*'

I took a chance and responded to that e-mail in an earnest, respectful manner, hoping this time I was on the right track.

At first communication with the mysterious contact was slow and took place only in small segments of communication. The source e-mail address changed several times until finally I was directed to what I will refer to as an internet 'back-channel'; a semi-secure place where messages could be sent or received in relative safety and anonymity.

I made no secret about the fact I was hoping to write a book on the Odin Brotherhood, to perhaps create something that built upon the work already published by Dr. Mirabello. I told them Dr. Mirabello had in fact thought it might be good for someone to expand on the subject with another book. As a busy historian and lecturer he had for the most part moved on to other areas of interest, I suspected. Yet like any dedicated academic he encouraged continual learning on any subject.

My contact seemed quite comfortable with the idea of another book being produced. In fact, I had the distinct impression there were those in the Odin Brotherhood who felt the time was right for people to learn even more about the Old Ways.

After a month of short, respectful answers to my queries, the content of the communications were giving me cause to believe I had indeed made contact with a member of the Odin Brotherhood. The nature of some of the answers given to me were, in some cases, both intriguing and surprising. Indeed, I cross-checked some of these with Dr. Mirabello, who on at least one occasion confirmed there were things in there he was aware of, but had not included in his book.

Based on this and other hints I concluded that my contact was of the Brotherhood or at least had some contact with them. I had no idea who this mysterious contact person was – and if indeed this 'person' might not actually be several different persons using the same back-channel. Yet all of the responses I received to my questions were informed, concise and dignified. There was a deep respect there I appreciated.

Eventually I was told to expect some help with the book I was planning to write. It was not long after that a mysterious, well-worn package full of notes with no return address marked on it arrived at my door. I had at no time given out my postal address to anyone.

The package looked as though it had been routed through several postal points of call and though the wrapping was well-worn and beaten the contents were fresh and revealing.

The materials I received were indeed intriguing. There was much there that had certainly not been included in Dr. Mirabello's book, yet I knew from further communication with the professor that in many cases the information in the package fit exactly with things he had been told.

It was more than obvious that they were well aware of my contact with Dr. Mirabello and others. I had a strong feeling that what I had been told earlier; that the time had come for those who wished it to know more about the Old Ways - was the motivation behind their generosity.

I knew what I held in my hands was a gift from the Odin Brotherhood themselves, that they had seen fit to allow me a tiny glimpse into their world.

And there was more. Several days after this, after I had spent some time going through the materials I had been sent, after I had spoken to Dr. Mirabello about this, I sent them a message that I had received the materials.

I received two distinct messages from my contact.
'We have given you the bones for your book. Add flesh.'
And: *'You may expect one day to be contacted.'*

2

A Voice from the Shadows

Rain poured down in lightning-illuminated sheets just outside the window-wall of the library's lower floor. Up the low hill and across the plaza from where I sat the grey stone clock tower stood like a lonely sentinel against the coastal storm.

It was late. I had been sitting in the library stacks for some hours now, sniffing through some books the reference librarian had tracked down for me. These were mostly books on old Nordic lore and on secret societies around the globe. I had been doing the groundwork for the book about the Odin Brotherhood based upon the information I had already acquired or been given, and was seeking any other references I could find in the stacks.

My contact from the Odin Brotherhood had intrigued me some time earlier with the rather cryptic statement: 'At times those who are interested or are of interest might find contacts to us in the pages of library books.' I had been keeping my eye open for the possibility of such during my visits there.

When I had entered the library the sun had been approaching the west over campus, though it had disappeared in a dark band of clouds approaching from over the Pacific. Rain had been in the air and I was happy enough to get inside before it hit.

The library had been busy. Students in abundance were crowded into various cubicles and carrels trying to get a leg up on upcoming papers. As an alumnus I had no such deadlines, only some free hours to do some research, though the quest for open work space had at first been a challenge.

Finally an open table appeared not far from the floor-to- ceiling glass wall which separated the wet verdure outside from the warm, glowing interior of the 'silent' study area.

I turned away and took notice that the stacks which had been full of busy students earlier were now largely deserted. I suspected perhaps most people had decided to take a dinner break. I looked at my watch and realized much to my surprise that the day was much further along than that. Buried in the pile of books before me I had completely lost track of time as it was nearly 9:30 in the evening.

I got up and stretched for a moment before returning to my

seat. Yet another flash caught my notice and I looked to see the main structure of the Old Main Library aglow for an instant in a white-silver flash.

Suddenly I felt a presence and without looking back I refocused my eyes on the glass to check the reflection behind me. I turned in time to see a fellow wearing a dark hooded pullover walking past through the carrels and tables. He disappeared into the stacks.

I went back to my reading. This lasted for about fifteen minutes when again I felt a presence. I was used to people passing close by in the study area as many of the spaces were relatively close together; the university was attempting to accommodate as many students as possible in that space and when it was full of people, a former classmate of mine described it as 'cozy.' I was not big on such 'coziness' actually, but one learns to adapt, as I had adapted during my undergrad years. Old habits had returned and I realized I had already dusted off the old 'mental shield-wall' I had developed so I would not constantly be distracted by other students passing so near.

'I see you are reading Mirabello,' said a nearby voice.

Indeed I had my copy of Dr. Mirabello's *The Odin Brotherhood* with me. It was sitting with the other books I was using.

I looked up and saw the person who had spoken was (I think) the same person I had earlier seen passing by in the reflected glass of the window-wall. He wore a black hooded pullover jacket and blue jeans. He was about the same build as me and had a stack of books underneath one arm. He grinned at me and gestured with his head toward my book.

'Have you read any of his other works?' he asked.

For a moment I wondered to myself if I should be annoyed at the intrusion, but to tell the truth I realized I was getting tired. I had been sitting in that spot for a good four hours and I doubted I had too much study-energy left in me for the evening.

'No,' I replied. 'Though I hear he has published some other books. I'll have to check them out.'

'This one is the best one, I think,' he said. 'It holds secrets.'

I was intrigued by this. Discounting the obvious fact that the book was concerned with a secret society, I had heard there were riddles of a sort contained within the book, mysteries that might be unraveled by persons who looked at them from the correct angle.

I told him that indeed I had heard tell of such things, although I had also heard many other things about the Odin Brotherhood at that point, many of them mere rumors.

'I have learned that rumors are sometimes the fair face of hidden truths,' he said. 'Not all, mind you, but some.'

I wondered at the odd discourse I was having in a near deserted university library on a rainy evening. For some reason I sensed certain irony in the situation though I could not entirely nail the feeling down.

'As you probably already know then, there are a lot of people who think the Odin Brotherhood is a hoax or perhaps some kind of social experiment made up by some university people.'

'Not everyone believes that,' he said.

'No, that's true,' I replied.

'Do you believe it?' he asked, curiously.

I looked up at him for a moment. There was something oddly familiar about him but I could not place it.

'You look familiar to me,' I said. 'Do I know you from somewhere?'

He grinned from behind his short, brown goatee. 'I don't know...maybe. I am a pretty common sight around these parts.'

He extended a hand. I noticed he had a very interesting looking silver skull ring on his right hand. It appeared to have a tiny, incised glyph on its forehead but I could not make out what that was. The ring looked old and well-worn and it glowed in the overhead light.

I saw no reason not to be cordial so I took his hand and shook it, introducing myself.

He hesitated for a brief second and then said 'Everybody calls me Crow so you might as well too.' He smiled again. 'Pleased to meet you, man.'

'Why Crow?' I asked. I suppose it would have been more polite not to suddenly question his identity like that, but it just slipped out.

'Why not?' he countered.

'Fair enough,' I conceded.

'Not my legal name obviously,' he added. 'But it's one I go by. I suppose I could have told you my name was Carl von Reichenbach, but somebody like you probably would have figured that out fairly quickly. Besides, that would perpetuate a myth I am not fond of.'

'What myth would that be?' I asked, innocently enough.

'That the Odin Brotherhood is some kind of folkish, Norse-Germanics-only club. That is far from the truth as you are probably aware.'

'Yes, I am aware of that,' I replied. I was aware of who Carl von Reichenbach was also. 'Well, Crow it is then,' I said after a moment.

He grinned and I grinned back. Any tension that had been present melted into the background.

'That is a cool ring you have there,' I said, changing the subject.

'Oh, this?' he replied, holding up his hand for a moment. 'I was given that by my uncle some time ago. He said it was to remind me that in death we see the value and sacredness of life.'

I recalled something someone had told me once that was very similar: 'We sometimes focus on the imagery of death to remind us of the value of life.'

'Very interesting,' I responded, nodding my head.

'*Post proelia praemia* and all that,' he said.

Indeed. '*After the battles come the rewards.*' I was familiar with that old Latin saying myself.

Another flash of lightning lit the soaking landscape outside, followed briefly by a rather loud peal of thunder.

'Thor is up to his business,' he said cheerfully enough. 'Well, it has been good meeting you, man, but I have got to go. Maybe I will see you around…and good luck on your book.'

I said goodbye, he waved, and in a moment was gone; disappearing into an aisle in the stacks.

'*Thor is up to his business,*' he had said. I was willing to lay odds he was also a pagan, like myself.

I went back to my reading but only for a moment. I realized I was too tired to continue. I thought for a minute about the fellow with the odd nickname. He had not looked Aboriginal and such a name as that seemed fitting for an Indian person to have, and yet I knew there were many people of mixed heritage who didn't necessarily appear nominal to the profile and expected appearance. Perhaps he had his nickname from another source? His ring looked like something a biker might wear, yet he didn't seem to fit that profile either. I decided not to jump to conclusions.

He seemed like a friendly enough fellow though. Perhaps I would ask him again about his name if I ever saw him again.

I paused suddenly. *How did he know I was doing research for a book?*

A library monitor walked through the study area then. When he passed me he said, 'Just to let you know, we are closing the library in fifteen minutes.'

I thanked him and began to gather my things together. I wondered what the guy in the hoodie meant when he wished me luck on my book. I had not mentioned I was writing anything so he must have meant good luck in my research or whatever it was he imagined I had been doing. I shrugged my shoulders and packed my books in my bag as they were already checked out.

Moments later I was out in the wind and driving rain of a storm that had been pounding campus for something like three hours solid. Such fierce storms were not overly common in the area and while I enjoyed the energy of a good storm myself, I was not overly excited about getting soaked to the skin on the walk over to the bus loop.

At last I emerged past the Student Union building and came

within sight of the bus loop. It did not appear overly busy from that distance, which at least was a relief. The university was a busy place in this season, as most such institutions are, and as mid-terms approached the crowds of students fluctuated with the exam schedule. It looked like I would at least be able to get on an uncrowded bus this time.

I paid my fare and took my seat. It was good to get out of the rain and as I looked around I was pleased to see there would not be too many other passengers on that particular bus.

The driver started the vehicle not long after I sat down and as we began to move I looked out the rain-splashed windows, at the water-refracted street lights and began to think about things. In particular I thought about all I had read that evening and indeed about what I had read in the package sent to me by a contact in the Odin Brotherhood.

One thing I had been told was this: *'We are few but we are everywhere.'*

I had pondered that much before and I found myself pondering it again. I began to wonder how members of the Odin Brotherhood could identify their own kind when they were so secretive. It seemed to me there must be some method for them to do this, especially if there were 'few' of them. I had asked this question of my contact once before and had received an answer that was ambiguous at best: *'There are ways for those-who-know.'*

Amongst the Aboriginal Canadian Native people I know there is a style of education known as Coyote-teaching. This is a method by which the one doing the teaching provides the student with just enough information about a particular subject to get them motivated and intrigued. After this the teacher supplies only ambiguous or even riddle-based answers so the student will go out and acquire the rest of the information or solve the riddles by themselves. It is thought that when a person is taught this way they will better retain and appreciate what they have learned, because something simply given has less value than that which is striven for.

I was not sure if the Odin Brotherhood had a particular name for their own mysterious manner of imparting or conveying information but I was convinced it was something very similar to the Coyote-teaching of the Native people. While I agreed with the premise of such methods there were times when I found them deeply frustrating. Those with whom I had contact in the Odin Brotherhood were, without a doubt in my mind, masters at delivering information in mysterious and often ambiguous ways.

I was further convinced that the manner in which they taught was specifically designed as a kind of filter: a method by which they might perhaps 'weed out' the genuine, respectful seekers from those who might have less than honorable reasons for their inquiry.

Whatever the reason, I had determined that in order to discover the things I wanted, I needed to do much of the legwork myself and also that I needed to ask questions from every conceivable angle. In my experience this was the best way to glean the knowledge I was after. The contacts I had were not going to make it easy for me.

Suddenly the bus made a strange noise, shuddered for a bit and then, as the driver pulled the vehicle to the shoulder of the road, it seemed to die completely. The lights flickered out and then came back to normal. The driver spoke on his phone for a couple of minutes before emerging from his seat cubicle.

'Sorry, folks, but it looks like this bus is going to be off the road for awhile,' he said regretfully. 'I have to wait for a repair truck, but there will be another bus along here in about half an hour.'

I looked outside. The rain seemed at last to be slowing down considerably. I asked myself if I wanted to go and stand at a semi-rainy bus stop for another half an hour in the wet, or did I want to do what my heart was suggesting and walk to the trailhead I could see along the road not far ahead and walk through the familiar woods and then follow the beach home? After some four hours sitting at a study table my body was practically crying out for exercise and although it would take me considerably longer to get home I thought the trade-off would be worth it.

I made sure my backpack was well sealed. I was also glad I had decided not to bring my laptop with me that day: I would not have to worry about it getting damp in the pack as I made my way along.

I left the bus and began to walk. In a few moments I had entered the forest where the trail was not all that difficult to make out, given that a nearly full moon was now peeking out between cracks in the scattered clouds.

The trail before me was down-sloping and quite easy to follow in the filtered silver light of the moon, and in less than half an hour I emerged at the other end, right across from the beach.

The formerly anvil-grey sky had fully broken apart now and had left large, star-splashed gulfs of clear sky through which the moon eagerly glowed. The surf was crashing in great, foamy waves and I realized I must have arrived at the crest of a high tide. A tangy, salty breeze blew in from the east filling the air with a fresh green scent and I knew I had made the right decision in choosing to walk rather than ride the rest of the way home.

In the aftermath of the recent rainstorm there were very few people about. The beach was largely deserted. I noticed a lone figure walking along some distance ahead of me, but this was the only person I could see anywhere around. He or she was not walking very quickly and so as I walked along at my own pace it did not take me long to pass them on the trail.

As I passed I heard a familiar voice say: 'Decided to call it a night, did you?'

I stopped and turned to look and indeed, although his features were now partly obscured by his jacket hood, it was who I thought it was; the fellow I had met earlier in the evening, the one who called himself Crow.

* * *

The walk back toward my part of town took over an hour and during that time I came to know the man called Crow a little better. We had been heading in the same direction, it turned out, and so we had decided to walk and talk. Crow did not speak much about himself and I noticed he stepped around certain subjects altogether; questions like whether he lived nearby or was actually attending the university received only vague, ambiguous answers and questions about his identity went completely ignored.

He was concerned about anonymity and he kept much to himself and while I respected that it gave me the feeling perhaps Crow was much more than simply a random person met in a library. That he was familiar – very familiar in fact – with Dr. Mark Mirabello's work, and he was a deeply dedicated pagan only added to the feelings of mystery surrounding him.

As we walked, once the pleasantries and initial identity-jousting were over, we settled into a most interesting discussion about pagan beliefs, particularly those originating in northern Europe, of the nature of secret societies and orders, and of course, the Odin Brotherhood.

At one point I joked he might be an actual member of the Odin Brotherhood come to 'check me out' though I would never know it. He replied to that by suggesting in that case I too might be a member of said order come to 'check him out.'

We shared a somewhat reserved chuckle at that. But in the end he said no, he was not a member of the Odin Brotherhood, but like he suspected me to be, he was a student of what they had to teach.

I admitted that, yes, I was very intrigued by the Brotherhood and that yes, I was eager to learn as much as I could about them. It was unlikely I would seek to become a member, though, I told him. As one who had long been fascinated with secret societies and also one who had been a pagan for many years, it would be enough for me to learn all I could about the Brotherhood.

'Which is why you plan to write a book about them?' he suggested.

I felt a sudden tingle up the back of my neck. I recalled my thoughts back in the library. I tried not to show my reaction and asked, 'How did you know that?'

He didn't skip a beat. 'Well, it made sense since you were studying all of those various books on secret societies and there was Doc Mirabello's book right on top. Also, since I know there are no courses offered on secret societies on campus I figured you must be researching for either a book or a paper of some kind.'

His reply was cool and measured. He did not seem to be lying and I am one of those people who is fairly good at detecting disingenuous behavior. So I accepted his explanation with a nod. It made sense and I thought to myself perhaps I was reading too much into the potentials of my mysterious new friend.

'It has been suggested to me that another book on the subject would be well received,' I said in answer to his initial question.

'Ah,' he said with a smile I could see in the shadows of his hood. 'I have also heard that. It would seem you have connections a lot like my own.'

Even though it had long since stopped raining, he had kept the hood on. He seemed to me to be the kind of person who was comfortable in the wrappings of anonymity. I wondered, perhaps only for a second or so before I dismissed it as unlikely, if he might be a fugitive from the law or something.

'I have one or two,' I admitted. 'They were not easy to acquire, let me tell you.'

'No,' he replied. 'They are very particular about who they will trust. I have had this experience as well.'

I could not blame the members of the Odin Brotherhood for behaving in such a way, either. A contact of mine once told me, 'Some think in terms of days, months, years or even decades. We think in terms of centuries.'

I could believe it. Things had not always been as open and tolerant as they were today, I thought. A society that had survived close to six hundred years, and no doubt more than a few attempts to remove all pagans from the face of the Earth, would be very particular about who they found worthy to communicate with.

'They are very secretive about some things,' Crow said. 'About other things they are quite open. It's the membership they are the tightest-lipped about but I think there are other things we don't know about.'

I agreed. Often the contacts I had spoke in riddles. I mentioned this experience to Crow and he chuckled.

'He rides a panther, black on black, in the low hills
by a misty river;
And even in the halls of allies he is often silent
Yet in his role he speaks volumes.'

'A poem?' I asked. It had certainly sounded like one.

'A way of describing a person who has helped me a lot on my quest for knowledge, particularly about the Odin Brotherhood,' he replied. 'I have found it is sometimes easier to describe such people in that way because their names are seldom known.'

'Oh,' I said. It was an interesting thought and an interesting way of looking at things.

'There are a lot of riddles within the Odin Brotherhood,' he said. 'The spirit of the trickster is pretty strong in there, I think.'

For a moment I said nothing. We walked in silence. In the distance there was a young man, out late, throwing a green tennis ball across the wet grass for his Irish Setter.

'So are you writing a book yourself or perhaps gathering information for your own reasons?' I asked.

'You don't look like a writer, did you know that?' he asked, dodging my question as easily as a fox dodges through thick underbrush.

'You don't look much like a crow either,' I replied. 'Crows are dark and...well, corvine, and you don't look much like either.'

'That's true,' he admitted with a chuckle, but said no more on the subject.

We continued our walk in silence for a few moments and then he said, 'I am thinking that one day I might perhaps undertake the Sojourn of the Brave. That's one of the reasons why I study orders like the Odin Brotherhood.'

'Ah,' I said. 'That would make sense then.'

The Sojourn of the Brave was the Rite of Initiation of the Odin Brotherhood. It was a three-day and three-night quest into the wilds where, after having been inspired by a potent dream and after careful preparation, the candidate would perform a sacred ritual. It was said that the Sojourn was a perilous undertaking and many had failed, but those who successfully completed it became not only members of the Odin Brotherhood but also oath-bound friends of the northern Gods.

'Have you made much progress in that?' I asked. 'In preparation to do the Sojourn?'

'Some,' he replied. 'Perhaps we can talk about that another time.'

We continued our walk, which lead us along the path closest to the crashing waves. Across the bay the moonlight shone whitely upon the local mountains. I recall thinking it would have been a fine night to have been up in those mountains, amongst the dark trees, around a cheery fire.

'I get the impression you are looking for as much information as you can get before you start actually writing this book of yours,' my mysterious companion said. 'Am I right in that?'

Crow had stopped in his tracks. He adjusted his backpack for a second but he was looking directly at me in a serious manner.

I stopped as well and said, 'That's true. And I get the impression from you that you might know a few things I don't,' I replied. 'One of my old mentors suggested I look into the Odin Brotherhood because he thought they had a lot to offer the pagan community and what we refer to as the Re-Awakening. Since then I have had it suggested to me that I might consider writing a book on the subject if I can find enough to write about.'

Crow finished shifting his pack and after a moment we began walking again.

'I have been at this awhile,' he said. 'There are things I would prefer not to reveal, but in other areas...yes, I will try to help you out along the trail I've already walked.'

I told him I appreciated his help very much.

'There are rules,' he said. 'The road you and I both travel is one that needs to be walked with respect. I have discovered many things and from what I have learned I know for a fact the Odin Brotherhood is very real. You know the saying by now, I am sure; '*We are few but we are everywhere?*'

I nodded. I admitted I had been pondering that very saying earlier in the evening, at the time I decided to walk down to the beach.

'It's true,' he said. 'When I started out on this road I had my doubts even though I hoped my doubts would be wrong. I have spent enough time at university myself to develop a critical eye and as you probably also know, attending a university is about so much more than getting the degree. It's about learning to be critical and above all, to know the system.'

I agreed. It was one of the eye-openers I had experienced myself near the end of my first year. The greatest successes were those who knew how to play the game.

'They watch, you know,' he added. 'I strongly believe once you draw enough attention to yourself, usually with enquiries and such things, there are those members of the Brotherhood who keep an eye on you to see if maybe you might be worthy of some attention. I know this because I have experienced that kind of thing.'

I told him that I too had done similar things to what he had described.

'Members of the Brotherhood could be anywhere; be anyone,'

he said. 'I mean, how do you know a professor or an employer or even a friend is not a member? There is no special way of acting or dressing as far as we know, and it has been said the Marks-of-Joy are to be hidden. The Brotherhood has been around for nearly six hundred years so I have no doubt they have gotten pretty good at moving invisibly in the world.'

'And that alone demands respect in my books,' I said. Though it was not unprecedented, six centuries of continuous existence was no mean feat for any association of human beings.

'Yes,' he replied. 'There is a lot of reason to go in with respect, the least of which is as you say, but also I think that if you do not go in with respect you will simply not be noticed, much less contacted.'

I suspected what he was saying was more than true.

'In some ways the order is like a time-capsule of lore and customs,' I said. 'But I believe there is much, much more there. I have used the analogy of the iceberg before when talking about this and I think the aspects of the Odin Brotherhood we are permitted to see are only the tiniest tip of that iceberg. There is a lot more underneath.'

'Yes,' he said. 'And because the Odin Brotherhood is cellular in nature there are probably a lot of icebergs.' He grinned, but only for a second before his face returned to a more serious posture.

'Many icebergs, yes,' I replied. 'But all made up of the same primordial ice.'

Crow nodded, obviously appreciating my analogy. 'And there is another reason why we must always go in with respect. I think there is a balance in everything and because of that, I think there is a sharp edge to the Odin Brotherhood for those who go in recklessly.'

'How do you know that?' I asked. I suspected he was right though; a tradition does not survive for nearly six centuries without having its defenses. Surely secrecy was not the only weapon of necessity in the Brotherhood's time-honed toolbox.

'I know because I have been told...and I have seen,' he replied.

The Odin Brotherhood has a saying: '*Strength over weakness, pride over humility and knowledge over faith*' yet I had also been told another thing: '*All members, though equal to one another, are superior to the rest of the world.*' Thus when dealing with the Odin Brotherhood from the outside, as a seeker would be, it was best to approach with respect. As my old teacher, Ari had once said: '*If you approach a bear with disrespect you can lose your life.*' The lesson was that in approaching something potentially greater than oneself it is always prudent to go in with respect...and more than a little caution.

For a few more moments we walked in silence. I think Crow was glad I had held my tongue on the questions that had threatened to spout forth in response to his last words. I knew that had he wished to elaborate he would have done so.

'Perseverance is also important,' he added. 'In today's world so many people want what they want and they want it now. They don't want to wait; they don't want to earn it anymore. In a true tradition things like even minimal contact must be earned.'

I agreed with that and told him so. The world was full of people who didn't want to put in the hours on anything anymore. As the population of mankind grows the search for individual uniqueness appears to flourish in some individuals and not in others. Some want to be seen as 'different' but don't really want to work at that difference – they simply want to announce that they are special...or perhaps buy it through association with some elite organization or group.

'There are a lot of liars out there I think,' he said. 'People who claim to have crossed the line-of-honor; completed the Sojourn. I think that more than a few people have claimed they are members of the Odin Brotherhood when they are not.'

'They want to feel special so they lie?'

'Yes,' he replied. 'And think about this: The Odin Brotherhood is a true secret society. They have been around for hundreds and hundreds of years and they have survived by staying hidden. Anybody who openly claims to be a member is instantly lying as far as I am concerned.'

I told him I had run across a few people like that; people who had made claims regarding not only the Odin Brotherhood, but of other secret organizations. Usually, in my experience, they were mostly teens or young adults trying to show the world how special they were without having to work for it.

Crow nodded in agreement to that. We walked a bit further in silence. The wind from the east was picking up, making the air a bit crisper. In the distance the city glowed like some kind of fairytale treasure; a multitude of sparkling colors against the deeps of the night.

'Even a hero becomes lonely. He searches for his own kind,' Crow said after a moment more, in a matter-of-fact tone from beneath his hood.

'What?' I asked. His comment had somewhat thrown me off. I had heard that before somewhere and after a moment I realized I had heard it from a contact I had. I quickly corrected myself.

'Yes, I have heard that myself.'

He grinned. I could tell that in his heart, this fellow was of a mischievous nature; his was a face used to grins, smiles and other such expressions. When I had seen his face in the library I could see he had a friendly but potentially trickster-esque face.

Every crowd had a joker and I suspected that this guy was one such – not in a malicious or mendacious way either. I had no doubt that his friends found him pleasant company. I found myself thinking that Fox or maybe even Coyote would have been a much more accurate nickname for him than Crow.

'So what would you like to know then?' he asked, breaking into my thoughts with a sudden cheerfulness.

'We could begin at the beginning,' I suggested.

'I will tell you what I can then,' he replied.

* * *

By the time I returned home that evening I realized I had been walking and talking for much longer than it normally took me to travel that route. When I had been conversing with Crow we had taken a few side routes on the trail and indeed had even stopped and stood around for periods of time.

Before we parted Crow gave me a telephone number where he could be reached and he asked me to use it only sparingly. I had agreed to that.

It was nearly midnight when I finally found myself at home, sitting at my desk and trying to get all that I had learned that evening down on my computer.

Crow had told me much and I could tell that indeed, as he said, he had been on the trail for a considerable time. He had learned things and some of that he had imparted to me on our long walk along the beach. As I typed I began to correlate much of the information I already had, in my mind, with the things that Crow had passed on to me. Already for me a number of gaps had been filled in. It seemed he had sources of information available to him that were different yet complimentary to those which I possessed, and I could see that when combined they made the larger picture much clearer.

I wrote down everything I could remember and I hoped I had not forgotten anything. I knew I would probably have to contact him at least once just to fill in the blanks of my memory concerning our conversation that night, but I didn't think he would mind.

My head felt overloaded. I knew I would need to sleep. I felt I finally had enough to begin putting my book together. Thanks to my own research, contributions by others, and now through this fortuitous meeting with Crow I felt I finally had enough to begin.

I had a lot to be thankful for. Meeting Crow had been the trigger; the motivational spark I needed to really put things in gear. I had been making contacts and gathering information for a long time it seemed, and all that time I found myself wanting; waiting for that extra little morsel of material I thought would be just the thing. I believed I finally had enough to go on. The next day would see the work finally begin to come to life.

3

Creed of Iron

Winter had come to the mountains. Across the bay the coastal peaks gleamed frosty orange-white in the light of the horizon-bound sun and I picked up my pace as I headed westward along the trail to my destination. At sea level the weather was milder and clear skies reigned over dry, pleasantly cool landscapes, yet the promise of chill drifted in the air like an untold secret.

Two months had passed since I had first met the mysterious man who called himself Crow. I had only sporadic contact with him through several text messages and two short conversations on the telephone. Otherwise I had nothing further from him. I spent a fair bit of time writing and along with tidbits offered here and there through my contacts I made some progress.

During this time I received a few communications from those who I considered contacts in the Odin Brotherhood. Naturally these came anonymously, through sophisticated back-channels and internet cut-out accounts so I never knew anything about the identity of the messenger. In reality I had never even been able to determine if my contacts were male or female but the value, as I had been told many times, was the quality of the information, not the identity of the messenger.

'*To protect our lore and ourselves, we keep our identities secret*' was something I had been told several times, along with; '*Our greatest secrets are the identities of our members. No one from outside who knows us knows we are members of the Odin Brotherhood. That is our way.'* I became used to the emphasis on keeping identities secret and after a time of frustration I simply accepted that.

The information I had recently received was a simple statement:

'*Because we are called the Odin Brotherhood, some women falsely see us as a male fraternity. According to our legends we were actually established by a woman, and we are open to women.'*

I was not sure what had prompted this. Perhaps it was simply to make a point, and indeed it was well made. I myself had wondered about the name of the Brotherhood in the beginning. It made sense they might wish to clarify that fact.

I had been told numerous times that women members were welcomed to the Odin Brotherhood just as men were. Indeed it made perfect sense because according to the founding story of the Brotherhood the tradition was started by the Shrouded-One-of-Odin; a woman. Other than that I was not sure of any details, such as the numbers of female members or what, if any, roles they might play, yet I recalled Mark Mirabello had mentioned the presence of women members in his book.

The Odin Brotherhood is, as I have mentioned, centuries old. The tradition, which began in Eurasia in the 15th century of the Common Era, was born of a horrifying tragedy which tore a small family apart.

The tale goes that a young widow, out in the wild honoring the Old Gods, was confronted by a depraved Christian priest; a twisted individual who demanded sexual favors in return for his silence in reporting her 'unlawful' acts. These unlawful acts were the acts of the widow being spied upon by the priest as she made offerings to the Old Gods.

The widow, known to us through the lore as the Shrouded-One-of-Odin, a proud pagan, refused this extortion. As a result, enraged, the priest turned the people of the widow's village against her. Ultimately she was beaten, maimed and brutally tortured in the name of the priest's desert god...and finally, burned to death upon a pyre of green wood.

Several years after the death of their mother, the widow's children communicated with her spirit which appeared to them from the Otherworlds. Based upon her instructions the process which would create the Odin Brotherhood was begun.

Indeed, the Brotherhood was in fact initiated by a woman. I was not sure why it was called the Odin Brotherhood in the first place by that thinking, yet I suspected those who originally named it thus had their reasons.

Thinking about that took me back to the beginning of my quest to learn more; back to the earliest days when I had only recently been contacted by the mysterious member of the Brotherhood.

A message said: *'Each of you has looked for us. Some of you have found us. All of you will know us.'*

I recall stating quite directly: 'You know I seek knowledge not only for myself but also because I have been encouraged to write more about the Brotherhood. I do not want to violate your trust by revealing things that I shouldn't be.'

The response was that, yes, they were aware of this and no one was worried about any untoward revelations by me. I was told there was a purpose to all of this.

'Chaotic times are coming. By spreading the lore it will not die.'

I was told it had been determined that if the presence of the Brotherhood was known there would be those who would seek it. If there were those who would seek it the lore would spread farther than it had done in centuries past. I was told that Dr. Mirabello's work had served a part of this purpose but there was yet work to be done.

The change is coming: indeed, it is nigh. Time is running short and the current atmosphere of tolerance in much of the world will not always be so.

'All time is a circle,' I had been informed. *'All time repeats.'*

In times past, I had been told, the Way of the Brotherhood had spread slowly and carefully, from person to selected person over the years. I was told that in the past a potential candidate would be carefully watched and then, if they proved worthy, they would be approached and communicated with by a member. They would be taught and indeed be instructed in the manner of crossing so they might self-initiate into the Brotherhood.

Yet it was thought there was a dark storm approaching and it was important to prepare for the potential of such a thing. There were those who believed a greater reach for the lore was needed and as such, in search of the worthy few, the Brotherhood stepped ever so slightly out of the shadows.

I recall asking once: 'Why now? Certainly this is a ruse that has been used by many conspiracy theorists or New Agers to promote some sudden 'knowledge' that they intend to foist upon the world. Aren't you concerned you will be lumped in with the crackpots and rip-off artists?'

The response had been thus:

'We think in terms of centuries, my friend. The petty trends of a few dishonest or crazed human beings do not overly concern us. We have weathered great wars and watched the rise and fall of countries and regimes. It matters not what some people think. What matters is that the lore is continued and that is what we do.'

At another point, on the same subject I was told:

'The contacts between men and Gods have been coming more frequently. Why is this happening now? We are seeing the fulfillment of Heinrich Heine's 1834 prophesy: *Thor leaping to life with his giant hammer will crush the Gothic cathedrals."*

Indeed, it appeared that a change of times was imminent and the Odin Brotherhood stepped from the shadows, even if only a small amount, to serve the role they were intended to serve.

These and many other thoughts passed through my mind as I walked along the seaside trail...

Two days earlier I had received a text message from Crow. It was, as I had come to expect of him, simple and to the point. He requested I meet him on the beach once again, at a location not far from where we had originally walked together.

As I approached the place, sure enough I spotted Crow, leaning up against a large metal sculpture near the seashore. I believe the large piece of art was intended to be an anchor, though sometimes it is difficult to tell with such things.

I walked up to him and he greeted me cordially. He was dressed much as I had seen him before: blue jeans and a black hoodie. Like before he carried his old, worn brown backpack slung on his shoulder. This time he wore sunglasses, the wraparound kind, and I could see myself reflected in the metallic blue lenses as I shook his hand. He suggested we walk and so we did, west, toward the beach trails that deviate away from the main walkways.

'Origins of the Odin Brotherhood,' he began. 'I have been thinking about that lately, especially since you expressed an interest in my beginning at the beginning...as far as what I know of the Brotherhood.'

I light-heartedly told him I had come prepared for our meeting and I had brought a recording device with me.

He smiled, although the smile was slightly more predatory than I had seen from him before. He asked me if my memory was fading with age. I grinned back and told him, no, it was not, but I wanted accuracy for the purposes of my book.

'Please destroy the tapes or erase the disc or whatever when you are finished. I'll ask that of you...and no pix or video, bro.'

I agreed. I told him I would be interested in hearing what he knew. I also told him that indeed, on my way to the meeting I was pondering the tale of the Shrouded-One-of-Odin.

'That is a tragic tale.' Crow nodded. 'But often powerful things come out of events like that.'

We walked for a moment in silence as we navigated a slippery section of trail. It swept down to the sand of the beach. The tide was on its way out so there were plenty of places to walk without getting overly wet.

'My experience began much as yours did,' he said, stepping onto the sand slightly ahead of me. 'I read a lot and I was initially urged to look into doc Mirabello's book by a mentor. I started to chat with people at gatherings and on the internet and eventually I was contacted. It took awhile as you well know.'

I did. As I have already mentioned it was not an easy task. Even as it was my contacts were anonymous and probably tenuous at best.

'And from those contacts my knowledge grew,' he continued. 'Life sometimes gets in the way of the best-made plans though, to get from there to here.'

We walked in silence for a time and then Crow said, 'We have many legends that cannot be confirmed by those who want to criticize and demand proof. Our legends pass largely by word of mouth.'

'What?' I said, thrown momentarily off guard by his comment.

'It's something my contact in the Odin Brotherhood told me,' he said. 'There are many legends and most of them have been passed along in an oral tradition. People who hear them and don't believe them might be listening with their ears but not with their instincts.'

We finally came to a large, dry-ish looking log sitting on the upper reaches of the beach. A high mud and clay cliff, overgrown with maples and oak brush, rose at our backs and a rather large family of crows scampered among the nearby rocks looking for food.

'I have been searching for a long time to find what I have found,' he said. 'I have learned a few things – more than a few things and I have made contacts. Some of them have been internet based...the first of them actually were, but also I have received communications via regular post as well.'

I recalled my own experience with a mysterious package delivered to my doorstep. The contents had been most enlightening.

'So a lot of my knowledge comes from people who have found me worthy of speaking to. Other knowledge comes from my research and even from practice.'

'Practice?' I asked.

Crow looked at me curiously, though I could not read his full expression through the mirrored lenses of his glasses.

'The Odin Brotherhood is based on three things, in my thinking,' he said. 'The first thing is that the lore is of the utmost importance. Keeping it safe and passing it on are crucial. The second thing is secrecy. I believe there is far more to it than the simple secrecy of the membership, but the bottom line is that secrecy is exceptionally important. The third thing is that the Brotherhood is designed to act as an instrument of Wyrd. One can get to know this Wyrd, or at least a piece of it, through ritual and practice. Through practice one can get to know the minds of the Gods themselves.'

I said nothing as he looked as though he had only paused in his talk. After a moment he added, 'So the practical application for those who seek to know the Old Ones up close and personal is practice. So many people stop at the books or at talk. They need to go the extra steps and those include getting out there and DOING, not just talking or thinking.'

'I see,' I said.

I could see where he was coming from as I too had incorporated a number of traditional practices into my life. Much had come from my grandfather and from my teachers, Ari and Max. Most of these were of an Odian or animist nature and as I came to learn more of the Way of the Odin Brotherhood I had applied some of what I learned as well.

'The Odin Brotherhood is a tool of the Gods,' Crow said matter-of-factly. 'It is a fraternity of Warrior-Sages or Shadow-Elites who serve a purpose in the Ørlog of our very world. This is not some gathering of tweed-jacketed old fellows carrying on in a comfortable lounge somewhere; this is a worldwide fellowship of very special pagan people who have an important role to play in the destiny of Midgard. If people like you and I wish to join this conspiracy of equals we have to work for it. It will not be handed to us. We need to make ourselves into the blade first and then, later, if we are worthy, the Odin Brotherhood will add the edge.'

He paused for a moment, as if deep in thought.

'You know I should probably add something about autonomy here,' he said. 'Kinda off track a bit but I am thinking about it so I should mention it.'

'Okay.'

'The Odin Brotherhood is all about individual initiative and individual contact with the Gods,' he said. 'Very early on I was told by a contact in the Brotherhood that people are largely programmed to look for hierarchy everywhere there is any kind of tradition, and with the Odin Brotherhood the emphasis for hierarchy is not there. Yes, we are aware of our standing with the Elder Kin; our place, if you want, but we are also told that within the Brotherhood there is no hierarchy.'

'Each of us is the captain of his own long-ship,' I added. I had been told that by my own contact not all that long ago.

'Exactly,' he agreed. 'Individual initiative and strength are very much valued and while I've been told that indeed members of the Brotherhood do gather and in some areas are known to one another personally, there is no **pecking order** per se; everyone is seen as their own Gothi and their own leader. It is the intrinsic way of the Odin Brotherhood to be like that.'

Crow took a breath. I could tell that he was thinking deeply once again, trying to get everything he had been mulling out in a way that pleased him.

'Think of it as a tradition where everyone is a chief of their own tribal Odinist nation: each a tribe of one. Occasionally these chiefs get together with others of their kind and hold what they call conventicles. Frith and mutual respect reign there so there is no need for hierarchies or any other kind of stratification.'

'So you are never, ever going to see a group out there advertising itself as the Odin Brotherhood,' he continued. 'Because of the model I just mentioned such groups can't really exist in the Odin Brotherhood way. If you do see such a group out there saying they are the Odin Brotherhood they are either delusional or they are outright liars.'

I recalled a little tidbit I had received from my mysterious contact. *"Those who claim to be us are not us."* I told Crow this and he nodded.

'Deluded or they are liars,' he repeated. 'Anyone who would claim to be the Odin Brotherhood cannot be of the Brotherhood because to make such a claim flies in the face of the reality of the Brotherhood. Also somebody who would do that is not showing proper respect to the Gods either: they are assuming they can pull one over on the Elder Kin themselves, and make claims of things they haven't earned.'

'Kind of dangerous games to play,' I suggested.

'Very dangerous and stupid games to play,' Crow added, agreeing.

Silence reigned for a moment. Neither of us seemed to have anything to say, and then Crow said, 'You don't have to be a Rhodes Scholar to understand there are powerful forces in the world; dark, manipulative groups who have been playing the nations of the world like patsies for years: whether it's some little group making false claims or the really big, bad guys out there. These big bad guys are by far the most dangerous: they want power over everything because they think their God gives them the right to it. The mainstream media suggests that ideas like this are crazy – that it is all some made-up conspiracy theory. Well, it's not, because the media bias is based in the Abrahamic worldview. That's what is out of balance in the world, my friend.'

I looked at him for a moment, not saying anything. His statement had been rather dark and foreboding.

'The Odin Brotherhood believes there are many Gods and Goddesses, many Old Ones out there. These Old Ones are from all over the place, not just the north of old Europe or any place else. There are hundreds if not thousands out there and the ones who count are about natural balance. That's why I think the Odin Brotherhood has allowed itself to become more visible over the past so many years; it's because they realize that a return to balance is more necessary now than it has ever been. They are an instrument of balance, like a sharpened blade.'

'And practice, such as ritual and other things will help us become this blade you speak of?' I asked.

'Yes,' he said. 'I have been told directly to go and make myself strong: strong not only in body but in mind and spirit. I have been told to learn to think differently, as a neo-barbarian, not as a domesticated animal. I go out in nature as often as I can. I spend time away from other people and I offer my honors to the Gods.'

'You have been told this directly?' I asked.

'In person as a matter of fact,' he replied.

I asked him to elaborate on that but he was obviously hesitant to do so. I did not want to appear rude or overly anxious about what he had said; that he had suggested actual physical contact with a member of the Odin Brotherhood – but the idea intrigued me considerably. I explained my thoughts on this to him so that he would not take my questioning as an offence.

To this he asked, 'How long has it been since you had doubts about the existence of the Brotherhood? Let me put it another way: what caused you to drop the cynical view so many have and realize the Odin Brotherhood is real and not something made up?'

I thought about what he had asked. I realized that I had a few doubts in the beginning. I had considered it healthy academic realism, yet the enthusiasm of my old teacher, Max, had lent considerable credence to the 'myth' of the Brotherhood from the beginning. Later, as I grew in knowledge of the Brotherhood, I eventually came to the conclusion that they comprised a legitimate entity.

'Quite a few years,' was my response to the first part of his question.

'So you most certainly don't view the Odin Brotherhood as a hoax or some kind of sociological experiment?'

'No, I believe it is a real entity.'

'And you don't think you and I are the only ones who believe this, right?'

'Of course,' I replied. 'I suspect there are quite a few who are either interested in the Brotherhood or are actually legitimate, initiated members of the Brotherhood.'

'Good,' he said. 'I would not be speaking to you if I thought otherwise, actually.'

Once again there was a pause. Crow picked up a small stone near his foot and tossed it into the sea.

'I can't get over how much crap is out there about the Odin Brotherhood,' he said, changing course. 'There are so many people out there with absolutely no lives of their own who spend every day at their computer picking apart the ways of others. It's ridiculous.'

I had seen my share of that and I told him about a few things I had seen recently involving the detractors of Dr. Mirabello.

'You know, the Doc is a good guy but he is not a member of the Odin Brotherhood, no matter what these idiots have to say. He's a historian who wrote a book about a historical thing. He has written lots of other papers and books about other historical things too and it doesn't make him a part of those other things either.'

I had to agree. I suspected in this world burgeoning with so much information available on the internet and in the media there was almost an overload. Some people simply could not cope with having access to so much. In some cases I suspected certain people had actually become delusional on the heady diet of conspiracy theories that abound on the 'net.

'Aegir is bringing the surf up,' he said in reference to the shift in the sea before us. The tide had turned and was beginning, ever so slowly, to rise over the rocks.

'I prefer the rising tide to the ebb,' I commented.

He nodded and threw another rock. Gulls, which had been feeding from the exposed rocks, leapt off as the surf rode in and were wheeling noisily above us.

'There are hundreds, if not thousands,' he said.

'Who?' I asked.

'Initiated members,' he replied. 'Think about it this way; there are close to seven billion humans living on this planet right now. What is a few hundred or a thousand compared to that?'

'You are saying there may be thousands of members in the Odin Brotherhood?' I asked somewhat incredulously. I had assumed that a respectable number had time to develop teacher-student lineages in consideration of the time the Odin Brotherhood had existed. 'There are those who have actually crossed over,' he said. 'Those who have successfully completed the Sojourn probably number in the hundreds, possibly as many as a thousand. There are also those who have begun the process of preparing for the crossing. Those may number in the thousands. I suppose I should have clarified that when I spoke.'

'And you were told this directly?' I asked.

'In a manner of speaking, indirectly, yes,' he said. 'Don't forget the members of the Odin Brotherhood will seldom speak in terms that most mundane folk would fully understand. Their words are for the wolves, not for the herd.'

'I see,' I said again. In my own experience as well, the members of the Brotherhood with whom I had exchanged information were cryptic at times; most times, actually.

A friend of mine, who has an interest in the Odin Brotherhood once, told me *'They very much enjoy puzzles and mysteries.'* I had heartily agreed.

'And indeed I have met one,' he said quietly. 'So they are out there, my friend. They are few but everywhere and if you play your cards right one day you might also have the experience of meeting one. Not everything is an internet chat as most believe: there are real people out there doing very real things, and the Odin Brotherhood is a very real thing.'

Questions surged once again, but I held myself under strict discipline. I did not want to push my luck and appear rude or ignorant.

The tide had begun to surge in with greater force and we were soon in danger of a good soaking if we did not move. As a result we got up and retreated further up the shore to a place on some rocks that looked as though it seldom felt the kiss of the waves.

'Okay,' said Crow, settling his pack down to the ground beside him and withdrawing two bottles of dark beer. He passed me one which I gratefully accepted. We twisted the tops off them and toasted.

'To those who know,' Crow said, and I answered with the same.

We drank. It was flavorful and refreshing and reminded me of the brew my old friend Ari used to make in his basement. Memories began to flow but I gently pressed them back into the recesses of my mind. I wanted to be in the 'now' while I was talking with Crow.

'Let's talk about the beginning then.'

I settled back on to my rock and listened.

'The Odin Brotherhood is about six hundred years old, but its roots are far deeper than that,' Crow said. 'If you look at the archaeological record you can see that the Old Ways of our people go back to the Paleolithic – at least in an unorganized sense. People can say what they want but our way is a very ancient way; a common sense, earth-way that predates a lot of what passes for religion or spirituality these days.'

I agreed. My old mentor, Max had spoken of this on several occasions. The ancestral people of central and northern Europe were far from the savages many in the past had labeled them as. Their ways were close to the Earth, yes, but they had sophisticated ideas and, even in the ancient times, tribal laws and ways of doing things.

'And a lot of those old ways persisted for a long time...until the coming of those other ways from the deserts to the south,' Crow said irritably. 'Then things began to change and most of the time that change was brought by force or sneaky political tactics. By the time of the founding of the Brotherhood most of Europe was deeply infected by the ideas of Christianity.'

At that last, he spoke as if he had something most unpleasant in his mouth. I could tell that when he thought of the era of the Shrouded-One-of-Odin, he was sickened.

'You know the story,' he said. 'The Lady was out in the green speaking with the Elder Ones when she was spied on by that priest.'

'It ended in her death,' I added.

A spark came to his eyes as he turned to face me.

'Yes, her physical death came, but little did that priest of the so-called white Christ realize what his criminal act would start. Ignorantly he triggered an event that would ultimately lead to the demise of his own twisted religion.'

I wondered about that. 'How so?' I asked.

'Do you notice they burned her on green wood, not dry, seasoned wood?' he asked. 'That is significant on a couple of levels. Firstly and obviously, the mob wanted her to suffer longer as the green wood burns much more slowly.'

'She may have died of her wounds or perhaps from smoke inhalation before the flames did her in,' I suggested rather hopefully. Anything to cheat the satisfaction of the savages who had put the Lady through so much already, I thought.

'That's possible,' he said. 'But what I was thinking about here was the significance of the deed as well. I don't think that the priest or any of his villagers realized it, but in fact the thing that was born of their crime is also like green wood: The Odin Brotherhood has burned for a very long time and like a lot of green wood you can only see the smoke, not the fire.'

It was a good analogy, especially after the Brotherhood decided to make their presence known through the work of Dr. Mirabello. There was smoke all right; the Internet was filled with rumor and supposition concerning the Brotherhood, but little else. One had to dig deeply and critically to get through the haze to what truth was available.

'Green wood reminds me also of mistletoe and that reminds me of the death of Baldur,' Crow said, shifting slightly on the rock beside me. He took a deep drink of his beer and sat further back on the stone.

All familiar with the tales of the Gods of northern Europe are acquainted with the tale of Baldur: Baldur, the handsome and fair minded son of Odin and Frigga, was given the gift of near imperviousness to harm by the magic of his mother. However, the only spirit of the worlds from whom Frigga could not get an oath of compliance was mistletoe, and though there are several variations of the tale, ultimately a spear or arrow fashioned from mistletoe took Baldur's life.

Mistletoe is considered a green wood by many, and thus in his words Crow also created another analogy.

'The cabals of the dead god think they rule safe from harm,' Crow added. 'But as in all things there is a fatal flaw and it is possible that, like Baldur, it may be something unexpected that ends their time on the Earth. To them green wood, wood that smolders hot and slowly, might also be the instrument of their undoing.'

It was definitely food for thought. The Odin Brotherhood was masterful at hidden meanings and puzzles. I had well come to know that. I thought it very possible that the story of the widow, the Shrouded-One-of-Odin, contained such messages.

My contact had told me, *'The poet named Poe said that the best way to hide something is in the open, with calculated clues of misdirection.'* I had discovered that in order to study the ways of the Odin Brotherhood, one had to be prepared to look at things from many different angles and to be ever vigilant for the appearance of subtleties and hidden meanings.

'Green is also indicative of that which is fresh and new,' I said.

It had been communicated to me by the Odin Brotherhood that their beliefs on age and corruption were clear. Green could also be indicative that the idea which became the Brotherhood was new and green, less corrupt than the way of the slaves who had killed the widow.

'And this fire on green wood we are talking about was set in the heart of Europe,' Crow said.

I was told the place was located in Eurasia. I could not discover any details beyond that. I told Crow this.

He nodded. 'I was also told this. It was called the Heart-of-the-White-Darkness. Doc Mirabello spoke of that in his book. The place was to the north of the Black Sea. A grim place to be while it was in the strangling embrace of Christianity.'

I had read that. Further, I had been told there was evidence which would one day be revealed that would confirm all of this to the world. My contact would reveal no more on that, however, than had already been revealed in the first Odin Brotherhood book.

'And the children of the widow were told by the one who had caused the death of their parent that they had to embrace the Christian ways or they too would suffer the same fate as their mother,' Crow reiterated. 'And these kids being fox-smart like their mom, perhaps more so, played the game; they pretended to be converted yet in their hearts they vowed to walk the road their mother had.'

Indeed that was the story. The children had never renounced the Old Ways and indeed continued to practice in secret. Between 1418 and 1421 they evaded the spies of their enemies and continued their traditions in secret. Finally, they were visited by the spirit of their mother and given the foundations of the Brotherhood. This was in the winter of 1421. It was a grim time but also a time of deep magic and the initiation of a powerful force into the world.

'The Odin Brotherhood was formed that evening in a ceremony,' Crow said. 'And from there it grew according to the rules the widow gave her children: three directives that have been followed ever since, for a very long time, in the shadows of the world.'

This was all in the book which had been put together by Dr. Mirabello from interviews with his contacts in the Odin Brotherhood: a conspiracy of equals was formed that would honor the Old Gods in secret places, and the traditions of this Order would be passed on, in secret, to those who were trustworthy. A league of hale companions was created where every member was a leader. A tradition of clandestine rites and rituals would be forged; the participants performing these were to do so in deserted places...That the knowledge of these things was to be passed on to the worthy; to those who could be trusted.

'But remember, knowledge is power when it is secret,' I said. I explained to Crow that it was something a contact had told me once. It was, next to the preservation of the lore, the very essence of the Odin Brotherhood.

Yet there is much missing from the tale. We are given the story of the widow and the things that were done to her. We are given the narrative of the children and the steps they took to communicate with their departed mother. We are told of the widow's return and the basics of what she communicated to her offspring. We know these things but there is much that has been left out: we do not know what became of the children, of the original folk who had been initiated; of the initial spread of the Green-Wood-Fire into the world.

'The conspiracy of equals has spread far, we can be certain of that,' Crow commented. 'They are certainly in evidence in many places these days and not just in Europe, though I am fairly sure that they remained in Europe exclusively for many years.'

I agreed with him on that as well. I had little doubt that there were members of the Odin Brotherhood all over the planet by now – and in places where they would least be expected, I thought.

'One day,' Crow said, 'The crimes that were committed, not only against the widow, but against all of our tribal people, will be accounted for.' He said that rather viciously. 'But in the case of that sacred woman, the Shrouded-One-of-Odin, our Gods created a weapon in her: a weapon that would one day cut the puppet strings by which a few hold sway over the many. It will be a weapon that bites deep into the killers of the world.'

When the Gods created man they forged a weapon. When they created woman they crafted a shield. I had heard this before, from one who is close to the Odin Brotherhood.

'What kind of a weapon are you thinking of?' I asked. I asked for the sake of attending to what he had said, but I already knew the answer.

'A weapon of knowledge and of waking up,' he replied. 'A long time ago a martial arts teacher of mine told me it was most unwise to leave a battle unfinished because your enemies will try to get revenge on you at a later date. The ones who think they have conquered the western world will one day realize that they did not finish the job, that they did not finish our ancestors off completely, and it will cost them.'

'Never leave a live enemy at your back,' I said. I told him that a teacher of mine had imparted the same lesson.

He agreed. And for a while we sat in silence looking out to sea. I thought again about what he had said about the analogy of the Odin Brotherhood and the burning green wood of the pyre. It made deep sense.

'There are others yet who think they might one day rule the world through subterfuge,' he added. 'They will find they are wrong in their imagined superiority. The world will change because the world needs to change. The ones who kept things out of balance will be left behind.'

I had been told, by contacts and other sources, that the early days of the Odin Brotherhood could certainly have not been easy, yet it was in those years of iron-winters that the value of secrecy would have been reinforced again and again. To breach the secrecy was to invite a slow, painful death, and no doubt the violence would extend to the members of one's family as well. In times when the simple act of holding one's own pagan traditions and beliefs was tantamount to a death sentence, the discipline of silence was a creed for the wise.

I recalled a tale told once by an elderly Norwegian man who had weathered the German occupation of Oslo during World War II. He had recounted how people very quickly learned the value of silence and that to keep one's mouth shut was a habit swiftly learned in those times. In silence there was power, so I was told, but also there was a measure of protection.

I had been told that the early years of the Odin Brotherhood were, to some extent, documented but that there are things which are not revealed outside of the fellowship. Because of the cellular structure of the Brotherhood there are probably a number of such sets of documents, all held in separate holdings. There was no doubt in my mind that there had been close calls as well over the existence of the Brotherhood. Indeed more than once had I heard references to the 'teeth-marks of Christianity,' and the 'ravages of the children of Abraham' in my communications with my contacts.

'What has happened before will happen again' I had been told in a cryptic e-mail once. *'It is for that reason we must be ever cautious in our secrecy.'*

As if gleaning my own thoughts as I sat there, Crow suddenly said, 'Those early years must have been terribly hard on the founders of the Brotherhood. I can imagine that they would have been hunted

71

down by the dogs of the church if there was ever a hint that they existed.'

He turned to me. 'So I don't know a whole lot more than you do on the origins of the Brotherhood, bro,' he said. 'But I do know that I like your iceberg theory. I think that the closer a person gets to the Brotherhood the more one will learn...but that will come only after the initiation. Maybe even not after that because to do the Sojourn is to become the friend of the Gods. You would need to do that in the right way to be accepted I think.'

'I think there are many filters in place that one must pass in order to get into a position of trust with the Brotherhood,' I said.

'Yes,' he agreed. 'There are a lot of spy filters and idiot filters too. Can you blame them? I can't.'

I asked him what he thought the true nature of the Odin Brotherhood was. I wanted to narrow it down and see if his ideas about it were similar to my own.

He sat in silence for a moment before he answered that one. 'I've commented on this earlier,' he said. 'But I think it's worth adding that it is the nature of the Odin Brotherhood to keep the old lore safe. And I also think it is the plan of the Odin Brotherhood to get its members into positions of power all over the place; from the smallest communities to the highest levels of government. I think that this plan is not a plan of greed or material gain. I think it is so that one day the world can be saved from the ravages of the creatures that have been killing her for so long. That is what I think.'

'Do you think that they one day want to control the world?' I asked.

'No,' he replied. 'I think they want to aid in the reawakening so that the worthy in the population – from all races and cultures – will wake up and realize we have all been duped by a relatively small group of people whose only desires are to take the riches of the world for themselves. A lot of people on the Earth have become no better than herd animals; they only think of their day to day lives and have no future. Some of these might be awakened, the rest will not be. The Odin Brotherhood wants only the awakened, enlightened few.'

'So, a few people in the right places can do much?' I asked.

'Yes,' he replied. 'The leverage of the wise outweighs the acts of a million lost folk.'

I thought about what he had said...

The Re-Awakening: I had heard that term before and not only from Ari. Many years later I had heard it from Max and others. It referred to human beings waking up from the stupor of the modern day globalized, industrialized nightmare that our planet has been turned into — to awaken and take control of our destinies as separate, yet equally respected traditions and cultures. The reawakening was about a return to the Old Ways as well; the ways where people respected the Earth as sacred and not simply as a resource to be plundered.

The worthy: another term I had heard in growing usage — especially with regard to the Odin Brotherhood. The worthy were the ones who had awakened and who were willing to walk the lonely road of the hero. I had also heard these people referred to as the awakened. These worthy ones were those dedicated to the deep pagan mindset and who were willing to stand as elite friends of the Gods, not as semi-mindless herd animals who were happy to be led by corporate and government masters.

The herd: yet another word in growing usage amongst certain pagan groups. It refers to the seemingly mindless hordes of human beings who are easily controlled by their respective governments, who have lost much of their identity and birthright as free persons and who are largely content to work, breed and consume.

I was reminded of something my old mentor Ari had told me. He had instructed me that people needed to awaken from the lie that all people were created equal. He had not intended this to be a racist comment, by the way, because Ari believed that all nations and races and their traditions could be worthy and beautiful facets of the world. What he meant was that among human beings as in all other animals there were those who were born to lead and those others, the significant mass of the population, who were made to follow.

My old teacher was of the opinion that the cabals who ruled the world had created many false impressions to dupe people into a false sense of superiority - so that they would be happy with their lot; satisfied with their day-to-day, mundane place in the herd.

'Give them the idea that they have no fences surrounding them and the illusion that they are free is maintained,' Ari had said to me once. 'Those of us who have awakened know better; we see the fence and we learned how to climb over it or dig under it.'

The Odin Brotherhood did not seek to rule: it did not seek to build fences. Indeed, for the few that it sought, those who were worthy – it sought to do the opposite, to tear down barriers and encourage the heady embrace of freedom.

'To rule is not our way,' had said a contact. *'Cowards and weaklings rule others. We master ourselves. By mastering ourselves we become lords.'*

My impression was that by becoming 'Lords' the members become a form of non-ruling aristocracy that I would say are friends of the Gods themselves.

'To serve is not our way,' I had been informed by that same contact. *'The Odin Brotherhood is not about equality either. All members, though equal to one another, are superior to the rest of the world.'*

I had considered on many occasions, in retrospect, that had he known of the Odin Brotherhood Ari might have sought them out as I had. His thinking had certainly been along much the same lines as those of the mysterious fraternity.

I had been told many times that the Odin Brotherhood has absolutely no interest in the ones who do not stand out as worthy. The ones who are content to be as herd animals are of little consideration.

As a contact once told me directly, '*We want the company of wolves, not the company of sheep.*'

I pondered that for a moment.

'The Gods are quite real,' Crow suddenly said, changing the flow of the conversation.

It is the belief of the Odin Brotherhood that the Gods are real beings, not spiritual energies or Jungian-style archetypes as some have mistakenly labeled them. As real beings who are neither omnipotent nor omniscient, the Gods of the North are dedicated to walking their destinies upon the Nine Worlds. As their younger kin, we human beings descended from the northern tribes are of interest to them as well. The Odin Brotherhood believes that the Gods and Goddesses take an interest in us and visit us from time to time, that they might aid or teach us...and as the time of the storm of change approaches it would appear their visits have become more frequent as well. The goal of one who seeks to initiate into the Odin Brotherhood is to become noticeable to these Elder Kin and, indeed, to offer them the hand of friendship.

'*The Gods of Asgard and other places are quite real*' as a mysterious person anonymously once told me. '*Our Elder Kinfolk walk the Nine Worlds regularly and upon Midgard Odin also walks – especially in winter.*'

I recalled one particularly informative exchange I had with my primary Odin Brotherhood contact. The contact had been speaking about the qualities of people who sought out the friendship of the Brotherhood.

'Thirty billion people have lived on the planet,' he had stated. 'Of that number perhaps there have been 125,000 who have exhibited special skill, enterprise or strength.' He had further gone on to say, 'It is from that elite that we draw our members. They come to us after they have been called by our Gods and Goddesses.'

It had been a most interesting exchange. I remembered it well.

'The Odin Brotherhood, in a nutshell,' Crow said, 'is there to maintain the lore of an elite cadre of warriors and sages whose goal is nothing less than to help save the world.'

He paused for a moment, watching me as if perhaps I might react as if surprised by what he had said. I was not, of course, amazed or surprised because what I had been told made sense.

'They have come out of the isolation and secrecy of a lot of years in order to teach what they know to the few who are worthy,' he continued. 'They want to keep the knowledge and wisdom of our ancient Gods and Goddesses alive – even if they lose the Earth to the herd and are forced to ultimately travel to other planets to do it.'

I had been told that before as well. I wondered if Crow and I shared the same contacts or there was simply a synchronicity of sorts going on. It was certainly not science fiction to believe that as an order that had existed for centuries and definitely thought long-term, the Brotherhood had not considered the possibility of its members one day traveling to human colonies offworld; there to preserve and teach the lore as well.

Crow reached into his bag and withdrew two more bottles of that amazing dark beer. He offered me another, which I accepted with thanks, asking, 'How many of these do you have in there?'

He grinned. 'It holds lots of different things though it doesn't look like it. It's the bag of the Dagda sometimes,' he chuckled.

He was referring I think, to the mysterious cauldron of the old Celtic god Dagda (Do-da), that was said to be ever-refilling by means of its magic.

'Not the well of Mimir,' I commented wryly.

'Not with too many beers in your belly,' he joked. He picked up a nearby stick and started doodling random spiral circles in the damp sand.

And we sat there for awhile; sometimes in silence, watching the sea come in, or at other moments speaking of local events – small-talk, basically. I made a point of turning off the recorder during that time. I did not think it was relevant. Crow noticed this and reminded me about our agreement: that I would erase the recordings after I was done with them and that I would attempt no video or pictures. It was, it seemed, of great importance to him and so, once again, I told him I was good on my word and I would comply with his requests. This seemed to satisfy him once again, and he soon launched in on a conversation about the fall hockey season.

Finally, after about an hour of the casual conversation – in which he very skillfully managed to say almost nothing about himself - he pulled out yet another duo of beers, which we duly cracked open in the crisp, sea air.

We drank.

'So,' he said, gesturing out to sea. 'You think you would like to know more?'

I felt a little tingle in my spine, as I recalled that cryptic message I had received from my first contact in the Odin Brotherhood, so many months before.

'Yes,' I replied. 'I certainly would. Whatever you have to tell me I would appreciate hearing.'

'Okay,' he said, standing up and brushing off the sandy legs of his jeans. We had finished up the beers and he put them in a separate plastic bag – no doubt for recycling.

He shook my hand and said, 'I gotta take off now but I will be in touch.'

And with that he turned to leave. At about five feet distant he suddenly turned with a grin and said, 'Next time drinks are on you.'

I agreed and waved as he left.

I returned for a moment to my seat on the rocks as I did not want him to think I was attempting to follow him. I waited a small amount of time before getting back up and starting on the trail home.

Crow was somewhat of an enigma and I wondered at the man. He was friendly and generous, yet there was something oddly familiar about him and much that was intriguing as well. Secrecy was important to him and I had worked to show that I respected that.

A glint of metal caught my eye and I realized we had missed a cap from one of the bottles. The surf was just reaching the perimeter of the rocks where we had been seated. I reached to pick up the cap. It would not do to have it washed into the sea.

And suddenly I saw there, amongst the doodles and spiral circles that Crow had left a single word, scrawled in the sand.

Önd

In the old stories, Önd was the breath of life given to human beings as a gift from Odin himself. Spoken of in the Voluspa, a work sacred to pagans of the northern traditions, Önd is thought to be at the root of inspiration and indeed, necessary for conscious life itself.

I could see the meaning in the word scrawled on the sand. Inspiration: it was the drive behind the Odin Brotherhood and the motivation behind Crow's quest to walk their path. The breath of life, through lore and deed, returned to its rightful heirs.

I watched for a moment more, as the incoming waves, dappled with white foam and littered in places with colored autumn leaves, washed the word away.

4

Of Gods, Goddesses and Other Elder Kin

I awoke suddenly from a very deep sleep and found myself sitting quietly, momentarily confused as to where I was or what I had just experienced in the dream state. I blinked and looked over to the large blue digits of my clock not far away.

3:04am it read; the hour of the wolf, as Ari used to say. It was that time between times in the early dawn where the potencies of men were said to be at their lowest ebb.

I sat for a moment longer in silence and recalled what I had encountered. It was a remembrance of a powerful dream I had experienced during the summer when I had been visiting my girlfriend at her home in the country. It was, I think, the first time I had ever re-dreamed a dream.

Since I had first encountered Crow in the fall, and since my research had deepened regarding the book, I had noticed that there were powerful things going on around me. Though I could not exactly put my finger on it, it seemed to me there was more energy in the air; my dreams had become more vivid.

Yet this was a dream I had experienced before I met Crow. It was most curious.

She had come in a dream...

It was a normal dream set; the usual swirl of contrasting yet believable worlds that most of us inhabit in the unconscious state. This time though, the dream set was interrupted.

The evening had been a late one. I sat with my Lady speaking of many things, deep into the night, as was sometimes our custom.

There was a storm, a fierce one.

Only two days earlier there had been such a storm as I had never seen before. Its roar was sufficient to knock plates from the counter in the kitchen and outside the lightning flashed shatteringly like actinic skeins of photonic fate.

Two days earlier I had given a libation; a Blot in northern pagan terms, to Odin out there in that howling fury. I had marveled at how my voice, raised high and loud, practically screaming, 'O-DINNNN!' had immediately been caught and swept away by the winds.

And on this night thunder crashed in massive peals outside, shaking the house as molten night-fire slashed in retina-burning fissures across the heaving grey sky. My daughter had come in earlier, frightened at the ferocity of the storm. She was happily asleep now, curled in a makeshift bed we had made for her near us.

At last our talk waned and the mists of sleep beckoned. We turned out the lights and drifted.

I walked in the usual discontinuity of fragmented thoughts and ideas found commonly in the dream-state. At once here, at once there, as thoughts of the day manifest in a seemingly physical form. It was certainly nothing unusual for me to have such mundane, fragmented dreams.

And then I found myself standing at a marsh. Behind me the darkness of a forest-wall; tall green conifers loomed grey black in the gathering dusk. A scattering of powdered diamonds flecked the indigo sky as the stars came out to grace the slow fall of a summer day.

Fireflies flitted at the edge of my vision, their tiny beacons flashing on and off; sometimes yellow, sometimes orange sometimes, more rarely, green. An owl hooted forlornly, somewhere out in the gathering mist.

Movement. Preternaturally fast, and a shadow suddenly appeared before me; coalescing slowly into the vision of a beautiful woman. At first I thought she was graced by flowing midnight tresses; long and lustrous, glowing faintly in the light of the crescent Mani, the Moon. Yet I think now her hair was in shadow beneath the hooded cloak she wore.

I may not be sure of her hair but her features and her eyes were startling: a face carved from the most feminine of dreams; soft, yet with strong brow, firm chin and high cheekbones, lips like summer rose petals beneath a nose which told of a regal heritage.

Her eyes; they were otherworldly. Imagine indigo and cyan together with the tiniest hint of violet in the twilight glow. Piercing, intense, on target, yet overflowing with a softness and wisdom not found in the women of my waking existence.

Was this a handmaiden of Freyja; of Frigga; a kinswoman of

Har? Was she a messenger of import from the land of my Elder Kin? Was she a bringer of knowledge or simply a fragment of my mind's desire for truth?

I did not know. I simply stood there in awe of her. I simply looked upon her and waited to see what she would do. I stood there in the almost painful, deep potency of the dream. Smells, touch, sounds, the air on the skin – all very real.

She spoke. I could not at first make out the words. It was as though she was speaking clearly and yet through the dreamscape the sound of her voice could not carry. Or was it that I was simply too thick to comprehend the words of one such as she?

'An....soooo.' That was what I first imagined it to be.

I implored her to speak again, and she did. The word sounded filtered, partially blocked.

'An...zo,' came the message once again.

There was a signal being transmitted, yet I was not receiving it en clair. I felt frustration rising up in me, threatening to turn to anger as I struggled to grasp the message.

She held her hands toward me; a marsh sedge, a reed, was held in her hand. It transformed from green-brown to black in the twilight, then to an almost actinic electric-blue. I strained to look upon it but it seemed to change shape before my eyes.

BOOOOOM!

I was jolted into the waking world. Thor Odinsson's hammer; the thunder, had pealed across the land with such ferocity that the glass shook in the window frames. I could hear the rain, in near horizontal sheets, striking the sides and windows of the old house.

Quickly I roused myself to check on my daughter who was soundly asleep, cuddled with her teddy bear; a gentle smile upon her beautiful face. My Lady was likewise unawakened by the onslaught of light and sound just beyond the walls.

I got up and walked the upper floor of the house, taking a brief respite in the washroom. Emerging, I looked out a window and gazed upon the flashing light show in the sky. I wondered if there might be a tornado warning despite my Lady's assurances to the contrary. I wondered if Mjolnir's might would be sufficient to hold the Thurses at bay this night.

And at length, sleep creeping back into my frame, I returned to my bed. I fell back to sleep almost instantly and returned to the seemingly arbitrary scenes played out on the stage of dreams.

But only for a moment.

For once again I was returned to the marshland scene. The mysterious Lady was waiting exactly where I had left her. This time she was smiling.

'An...zo,' came once again from the mind and voice behind those wondrous lips, guided by those otherworldly eyes.

Once again I struggled for comprehension, for meaning. It would not come.

CRASH!

I snapped awake yet again. A thunderous peal rumbled across the house and bounced back into the night. Downstairs my Lady's hound grew restless and began to whine.

I waited, lying in silence and waiting to see if the disturbance would continue. After a few moments it seemed to me as though the maelstrom was coming to an end for the night. Again I drifted back to sleep.

This time I did not drift back to the land of disjointed scenes. This time I returned directly to the marshlands, where I realized time had passed regardless of my presence there. When I had first gone to that place the shade of twilight was falling gently across the fen. Now the place was touched by the fullness of deep night. Sounds had changed, the owl no longer hooted. Somewhere a coyote or wild dog barked. Crickets sang their synchronous susurration across water and reed – now glittering in broken moonlight driven by a brisk, cool breeze.

And the Lady was still there, wearing an expression that no

doubt was usually reserved for the training of small children; calm and collected but with a certain hint of impatience.

She said the word again, and again she held the transforming blue-black reed before her. She grinned as she looked into my eyes and saw the growing apprehension there.

She spoke again, this time in clear English. Her voice was like the song of a small creek chuckling over round stones in the bright, midsummer sun. It held the gladness of small children at play and the softness of an Elder's voice all in one crystalline package.

'You will know,' she said softly. 'Now do something with what you have learned.'

And I saw the image of the reed; of the colors ever shifting within it, always returning to blue, a blue not unlike the Lady's enigmatic eyes.

And I slept.

The scene was gone; the place that had been so very, viscerally real, was gone. Yet in my dreams I heard the voice over and over again. I heard the word that I had not been able to grasp.

Again and again I saw the reed; the shape changing reed.

At last the reed settled into shape, like that of one half of a barbed spear.

At last the voice stopped and the sound I had been attempting to discern faded to silence.

I awoke. Dawn had long since flooded in past the drapes and was creating long, vertical bars of light upon the floor and one wall. I sat up and checked on my daughter who was still fast asleep. My Lady was not there; she had arisen before us and had left the room.

I sat in the semi-darkness and pondered. Thoughts came back to me and I saw myself in my mind's eye, sitting on a large, grey stone, somewhere far in the hills. I looked around at the forest spread below me, flowing like green rivers to the ocean far below. Somewhere in the hills a horn sounded. It reminded me of the sound of an ancient Lur.

In my mind's eye the scene wavered and I returned to the present moment, sitting on the edge of a bed in the semi-darkness.

ANSUZ.

That was the word; THAT was the message.

The name of the Ancient Germanic rune.

It had been a hard message to transmit it seemed. I had no doubt the reason for this was that I was a difficult recipient; I had at first not been prepared for its receipt. Yet the message had been delivered.

And I pondered there in the darkness yet longer. I recalled the words of a man named Walker Kale. Walker had been a friend of my grandfather's and was a man known for his deep wisdom. He had told my grandfather and others many things, and one of these things he had spoken of was his advice for the Warriors and 'the ones who know.'

Like my grandfather and indeed, much like Ari, Walker Kale believed in the necessity of keeping the Old Lore close, of protecting it from the erosion of the world. He believed that men and women, sacred and special to the Gods would be needed to keep that flame of truth in deepest night so that human kind would never forget that there was a beautiful world beyond the miasma presented by the followers of the Cabal and their power-hungry Masters.

He said, *'Live quietly in the hollows of the world: a flame of truth in deepest night.'*

And I had seen similar things of late: potent things, powerful things, especially since I had made the acquaintance of Crow.

I realized that indeed I had been living in the hollows of the world and during the night I had come to understand the second part of that message. Things were becoming much clearer to me as time went by.

It was then my phone, sitting on a nearby table, chimed. I realized I had forgotten to turn it off for the night as I usually did.

I flipped it open and read the text message that was waiting. It was from Crow. It read, 'Check your e-mail.'

For a few moments I resisted going to my computer. I felt weary from the dream I had re-experienced, even though the second experience lacked the power of the original one. The recent dream was almost a review of a dream rather than a dream itself, yet the message had carried a substantial energy with it. I felt tired out simply from having experienced it.

Finally curiosity got the better of me and I went to my computer. I opened the message from Crow and it requested my presence at a certain location in three days' time. The location was a considerable distance from the city and the message told me to be prepared to camp.

I replied, telling him I would have to check my schedule, even though I knew full well I would make the time. I had not heard from him at all since December. It had been nearly four months and I thought he had simply disappeared. In the short time I had known him I had come to accept this kind of behavior on his part. At times his messages would simply appear, with little warning, just as he seemed to pop in and out of my world at unexplainable, unpredictable intervals. I had the impression he did not have to work very hard at being mysterious; he lived the role quite naturally.

I turned off the computer and returned to bed, hoping to spend the rest of the night in relatively uninteresting dreams.

* * *

'Behold my friend; the crucible of stars!' Crow said from his place at the small fire. He had not risen but raised his arms skyward in a grand kind of gesture.

I was quite tired, yet I earnestly appreciated the deep bowl of night. It had smoothly flowed into place above us following a spectacular pink-orange sunset. It was late March and in the mountains the chill kiss of winter was still far from faded; yet the black, clear sky overhead, made clear by the cold, was indeed a splendid canvas for the emerging stars.

It had been a goodly amount of work to get to where we sat, camped near some trees at the base of the slope. We were in a deeply sacred place that held a lot of power, not far from the traditional lands of the Squamish First Nation, about fifty kilometers from Vancouver.

I had met Crow at the side of the highway as he had requested in his message, and we made our way to the trailhead after a long journey. The trail we followed was steep and in many places wet with melting snow. Indeed there was still much snow in many places: the local creeks roared with melt-water from the peaks above, lending the air a bright, refreshing, if not chilled, feeling. It was slow going for a considerable distance and during this time, unlike our usual meets, we spoke very little.

Several hours later we had finally made a small camp on a rise between two descending slopes. This had happened none too soon either, as the sun had been rapidly approaching the horizon as we got into our camp. In the mountains – especially in the darker seasons, night comes rapidly and so we made haste in setting up our small tents and gathering what firewood we could find around us.

Finally, fed and somewhat relaxed, I found myself seated on a log around a small fire in deep, descended night.

'I was thinking that we could talk uninterrupted while we are here,' Crow said.

'What did you want to talk about?' I asked.

Crow was suddenly quite animated. It was the opposite of the mostly silent, determined attitude he had shown throughout most of the hike. I wondered about that silence but had thought it to be a kind of deep thought or meditative manner and had not questioned him on it. I had known several others over the years who had adopted a similar mannerism while hiking.

'The ones that many call Gods or Goddesses are quite real,' he said, poking a stick into the fire. He had spoken of the Gods like this before. 'They can appear to be quite solid. They are not see-through ghosts or figments of the imagination. They do not exist only in our heads or in some symbolic, Jungian style way. That's not my way of looking at them and it is not the way of the Odin Brotherhood either.'

He paused for a moment, looking at me seriously, and then he reiterated, 'The Old Ones; the Gods, are real. They come to this world often.'

I agreed with him. It was my belief also that the Gods were quite capable of coming into our world and visiting in solid form. Unlike the Gods (singular or otherwise) from some of the other belief systems, our Gods were not omniscient, not omnipotent and were not immortal in the generally accepted meaning of the term. The Gods of our people, the Gods of those who considered themselves to be pagans of the northern paths were subject to the laws of nature in their own way.

I recalled a conversation I had experienced, many years earlier, with my old teacher Ari. Ari had been similarly animated when he spoke of the Elder Kin:

'They are like us, yet not like us,' Ari told me. *'They are like us in that we are their kin; and we are descended from their ancient bloodlines, but still we are to them as children. They are vastly beyond us and we should never forget this.'*

This view of the Gods, or Elder Kin as I had come to call them, was one of the things that had drawn me to study the ways of the Odin Brotherhood as they too believed the Gods were real and that they visited the Earth. Many pagan people I knew did not subscribe to that view. In fact many perceived the Gods in ethereal or even metaphorical ways. I was not given those ways in my own tradition though: like the folk of the Odin Brotherhood I saw the Gods and Goddesses as being solid and real.

'So I assume, then, you wanted to talk about the Gods and Goddesses?' I asked.

He grinned. 'The Gods and Goddesses and the other people of the spirit realms too.'

I nodded in as sagely a manner as I could.

He said, 'Not much point in going over the names and roles of individual Gods. You know who they are and the stories associated with them. What I am most interested in is talking about the nature of the Old Ones.'

I could see his point. I suppose it would be repetition to review the names and roles of the Gods of the North here. Most people who are familiar with the old stories will also be familiar with things like Odin as the wandering sage and Warrior; Thor as the thunderer and protector of the common man, etc.

Crow got up and went over to his pack, which was propped up against a tree near his tent. After a moment he returned bearing two frosty-looking brown bottles. They had obviously chilled considerably as the night had descended. I remember thinking that if he ever got tired of his current name he might change it to something which described his beer-purveying abilities.

I grinned at my inner thoughts and he grinned back.

He opened both bottles and handed me one. 'This is pretty potent stuff so go slowly. It'll warm you up though.'

I accepted, telling him I too had brought a few bottles with me. I had not forgotten our last meeting and I had determined to keep my end of the beer-bargain.

'Good,' he said. 'A few beers in good company are good for the spirit, I think.'

I looked at the bottle in my hand. It amused me to note that the label had a picture of Odin on it. He was holding a foaming horn before him and smiling craftily.

'Odin's Tipple, eh?'

'From Europe,' he explained. 'Hard to get but worth the search.'

We toasted and I sipped. It was deep, rich and potent.

Over the next few hours, in the deepening night, we talked. Crow was intensely animated by this subject, as I have mentioned earlier. I sat and for the most part listened, interrupting only to ask a question or to request clarification. Crow spoke with passion about the Gods and also about the way the Gods were viewed by the Odin Brotherhood.

I asked him several times where he came across various bits of what he knew – particularly when that information pertained to the view of the Odin Brotherhood. In each case he told me his information came from two sources: his contacts with the Odin Brotherhood and his direct experiences in the wild places; direct interactions with the sacred.

'The Gods of the north as perceived by the Odin Brotherhood are not quite the same as the Gods that many northern pagans believe in. I thought even though we are talking about the nature rather than the identities of the Gods, I would mention that,' Crow said after taking a deep drink of his beer. 'Most modern pagans are simply sheep trying to act like wolves yet underneath the disguise they are basically still behaving as Christians or even Wiccans or whatever they were before they came to the Old Ways of the north.'

He sat back for a moment and regarded me. I suspected he was observing me to see how I would react to his statement. I remained neutral and attentive.

'Several of those who instructed me over the years thought similarly,' I said. 'We live in a soft world and it is difficult for many to completely walk away from the old teachings or the way they were brought up. I myself took years to get completely free of the ways of my Protestant upbringing. It's not an easy thing.'

'No, it is not an easy thing,' he said, seemingly satisfied with my response. 'I fought long and hard to escape the programming of my childhood too.'

I had a feeling that Crow could be quite a dangerous person if he wanted to be. He had that kind of primal edge about him – as though he was a piece of dark nature given human form. In some ways he reminded me of a younger version of my late grandfather who had exuded a similar energy.

'The Gods of the north as perceived by the Odin Brotherhood are not quite the same as the Gods that many northern pagans believe in,' he reiterated. 'They are not worn smooth by modern political crap or the manipulations of an overly clever media. The Gods of the Odin Brotherhood are hard and sharp. They are the Older Kinsmen of an elite human cadre; a hidden aristocracy of Warriors and heroes who dare to fare forth in ways unimaginable to a herd animal.'

There was a razor edge in his voice, one that spoke of strong emotions simmering just below the surface. I had a feeling that Crow had experienced some grim things in his past that led him to his current views. I decided not to ask about such things as I thought he would explain them to me if he wished.

Crow seemed to catch himself there; seemed to realize that his underlying emotions were perhaps clouding his otherwise clear night and for a moment he sat back again, taking a small sip of his brew.

My thoughts took me back to my old teachers, in particular Max who taught that the Old Gods were not to be trifled with; that they could be capricious and dangerous with those who showed a lack of intellect or respect.

I also recalled once again the comments by Ari concerning the edge beneath the surface on the Elder Ones: *'Even the lovely and compassionate Idunna, or the wise and matronly grandmother Frigga will tear your head off without the slightest hesitation — in an instant — if you cross her the wrong way.'*

Words I remembered from many years ago. They still held the same power for me that they did back then. They were words of advice and words of warning. They expose us to the reality of our Gods, caution us to respect and tell us that when we are dealing with these venerated folk we need to do so in the fashion of a person approaching any respected Elder.

In the way I was taught, and I could tell it was a way similar to that which was passed on to Crow: the way of the Old Ones is not the way that most modern pagan people are taught. My teachers had the experience — the intimate experience — of dealing personally with the Elder Kin. They took lessons directly from the source with no intermediaries and they passed on what they knew with as little interpretation as possible so as to retain the authenticity of the message.

I looked back to see that Crow was satisfied in his silence for the moment, staring into the orange embers of the small fire. I went back to my own silence of thought...

I am reminded of a story within the traditions of the Odin Brotherhood given to us by Dr. Mirabello in his book which tells of the sage called Innocent-of-Conviction and his quest to discover which of the deities were worthy of the highest honor. In this story we hear him relating to three groups of godly beings, but as all true pagan people know there are thousands if not millions of beings that we of Midgard sometimes call Gods.

In the tale, Innocent-of-Conviction approaches the being known as Yahweh by some, and called him a cruel and ill-tempered despot. The so-called desert god, true to form, erupted in a fiery rage and bullied Innocent-of-Conviction into silence.

Innocent-of-Conviction then sought out another one, the 'pale and dwarfish' one who was called The-God-Who-Fears-Oblivion-and-Neglect. Innocent-of-Conviction called this being to task by saying that anyone born in an animal shed certainly did not smell like a God.

As expected this individual chastised Innocent-of-Conviction but in the end forgave him ever-so-loftily.

Finally Innocent-of-Conviction made his way to the halls of the northern Gods. There he encountered a group of our Elder Kin enjoying a feast of pork in a high hall. The sage tested these Gods by suggesting to them that they were false Gods who satisfied lusts and procreated monsters.

One of the Gods, displeased by this, warned the sage, telling him that if he was forced to draw his sword he would not sheathe it without the sage's blood upon it.

To this the sage, Innocent-of-Conviction, declared that he had found courage and that a brave man did not fear the wrath of Gods.

Rather than be further angered by this statement the Eddaic Gods found deep appreciation in the sage's words, so much so that they laughed and invited the sage to join them in their feast.

There was a moral to this story and this is that one should beware of Gods who cannot laugh.

Thus ended that tale and I will say the first time I read it I was astonished by the courage of Innocent-of-Conviction, at the temerity with which he approached beings far more powerful than himself and the dedication he placed in his quest: to find knowledge or die trying.

A voice drew me from my reverie and I realized Crow was speaking to me. He was grinning again, all dark clouds gone from his visage, and he was commenting that I appeared lost in thought. I told him I had been thinking about the tale of Innocent-of-Conviction.

His grin widened. 'You understand,' he chuckled. 'Many do not, bro. Many don't get that.'

I reached over to put another stick of semi-dried wood on the fire. It smoked and popped a bit at first, but then warmed and was taken in by the blaze.

'The lesson of Innocent-of-Conviction is obvious to those who know and even fairly evident to those who want to know. It is not just about watching out for Gods who can't–or won't–laugh, it's about the very nature of our Gods and Goddesses. They are not the kinds of Gods that modern western society has come to expect. They are not wispy little fairy-people nor are they all benevolent old dudes who live on clouds. They are real and they are hard. They are part of nature: REAL nature with all of its storms, teeth and claws.'

'And the tale of Innocent-of-Conviction tells you that?' I asked.

'It tells me way more than that,' he replied. 'It tells me that while our Gods can be harsh and deserve respect they can also be fair and even friendly. Don't forget that we are their younger kin: we were designed to be like them and should aspire to be like them, not like whiney little monkeys who live in cages and fear the woods or the night.'

He looked squarely at me from across the fire. 'The Odin Brotherhood teaches us to be like Innocent-of-Conviction. He is a role model, a hero-sage who is not afraid to get his hands dirty and not afraid to venture into the dark and not afraid to stand up and be heard. Innocent-of-Conviction challenges preconceptions and he holds no man-made laws as his own. He is a little piece of the Gods himself and he laughs at the ridiculous rules that are made up for sheep. He is elite. He walks his own way and he tries to be as much like his Gods as he can.'

I thought about that. It made a lot of sense and indeed it chimed with much that I had been taught. Why did the fearsome Eddaic Gods not slay Innocent-of-Conviction on the spot for his confrontational words? This too is simple, and on multiple levels: they are not as we are; they have never been part of a slave culture and they think as wolves, not sheep. To them strength and brazenness are appreciated. To them directness is valued. They respect those who are like they are.

Innocent-of-Conviction had proven himself worthy to these Elder Kin. He proved to them he was no real threat and he had a strength that they respected. All we have passed along to us is the tale; we cannot see the body language that was used—we cannot feel the energy in the air. We do not know, fully, the depth of character which Innocent-of-Conviction brought boldly into that hall but we have the essence of the moment brought to us and I am sure that can be appreciated by those who know.

Approaching our Elder Kin always carries with it some level of risk. I believe that this is a good thing, too, as only the worthy should approach our Gods and Goddesses. And who decides exactly who is worthy and who is not? Our Elder Kin do, naturally.

The stated moral of the Innocent-of-Conviction story was 'Beware of gods who cannot laugh,' but it is also a cautionary tale as far as I am concerned, one that tells us to be wary about our own worthiness when we approach the Elder Ones.

Our Gods are beings of the icy north, of black forests and rugged mountains and fields of war. They do not come from the relative comforts of the desert lands or from the viand-dripping paradises of some of the eastern spiritual traditions. As such their ways are harder, darker and much, much sharper than what most of us western-worlders have been led to believe. So very many pagan folk I have met make potentially lethal mistakes, several actually, when interpreting the nature of our Gods and Goddesses.

The first mistake is made because so many have allowed the influence of their (probably Abrahamic) upbringing to seep into their perceptions as a pagan. When this happens the Gods often become viewed as ethereal, unreachable, all-knowing immortals whose wisdom can only truly be translated to us through a trained intermediary class, such as priests or Gothar. All this does is isolate us from the reality of our Gods and Goddesses, transferring control of what is known and what is not into the hands of a priestly class.

A second mistake is made when modern-day pagans begin to rationalize the Gods according to modern-day preconceptions or processes. When this happens the Elder Kin become specimens to be analyzed and dissected along psychological, metaphysical, or social theory models. Like the first mistake I spoke of, we distance ourselves from the Gods when we start imagining them to be internally generated avatars, Jungian archetypes, or unknowable energy forms.

Even worse are those who are what I refer to as 'Lazy-pagans': those who seek to be cosmic consolidators and begin labeling our Gods and Goddesses as simply aspects of a dualist Lord and Lady concept or even more atrociously, simply many faces of a single godly entity. Like the first mistake, this way of dealing with the Gods is at best an isolationist approach and at worst has the potential to transform us back into the very fawning sheep-folk most of us fought hard to escape in the first place.

A third error, and possibly one of the more egregious ones, occurs when a pagan person comes into the mindset which leads them to believe our Elder Kin can be dealt with on a casual, almost laid-back way. Too many times I heard people referring to the Gods in this informal context–making comments such as, 'Oh I'd love to hang out with Odin,' or 'I'd have a beer at the bar with Uncle Thor,' or even 'I wouldn't mind a raunchy night with the lovely Freyja.' Comments and attitudes like this simply radiate ignorance of the nature of our Elder Kin and, indeed, ignorance of where one stands in relation to them. This is not to say we should bow and scrape before our Gods and Goddesses, or that we should be so formal as to not be open to clear communication from our Elder relations, but it is crucially important that we are aware of the fine line between respect and disrespect. Understanding the nature of the Gods and Goddesses is an important aspect of the way in which we approach them.

'Be heard but not herd,' I ventured.

Crow got the word-play.

'I am stealing that.' He chuckled.

'The bottom line is what I like to call Kin-Bond,' Crow said, placing yet another piece of wood on the fire. The chill of night had now crept further in and we could feel the cold as the fire burned down.

'The Gods prefer their own people,' he said. 'And when we learn the lessons taught to us in the Eddas and in stories like the one about Innocent-of-Conviction we are given clues about how to behave properly. When our Gods see us behaving properly they will be more likely to make more contact with us because it is an increase of Kin-Bond, that connection of family we have with them.'

'Their own people?' I asked. 'Can you clarify what you mean by that?'

'Sure,' he said. 'The Odin Brotherhood believes there are many of those beings we call Gods and Goddesses. Not all of them are the Gods that a Norseman or an ancient German or Celt would recognize. There are Old Ones who seem to have shown a preference for the humans of other lands – the Gods and Goddesses of ancient Egypt or Sumeria or China, for instance. A lot of these Old Ones tend to favor a specific group of humans, though this is not always the case.'

'You mentioned behaving properly a minute ago?' I asked, more to play trickster's advocate than anything else.

Crow got my meaning and laughed again.

'Behaving properly is not that difficult...well not that difficult for some of us,' he said. 'It is behaving in a manner that our Elder Kin will appreciate. It is to behave like they do: to be like wolves or bears or coyotes or hawks and ravens, not like herd animals. The Hávamál nails it down pretty well in fact. Behave tribally, like a member of a Warrior family and you are behaving properly.'

He paused for a moment, poking at the fire.

'The Odin Brotherhood has a saying,' he said. 'In any situation, what action is required? What is born of weakness is bad. What is born of strength is good.'

I nodded and took a drink of the brew he had given me. He was right: it was potent and indeed it did impart a warming effect, something that came in handy in the chill where we camped.

'People think the Odin Brotherhood is an ethnic movement, kind of like Asatru or what many term Odinism, but the Brotherhood is not actually like that,' Crow said. 'When a person initiates into the

Odin Brotherhood they become literal blood-brothers of the Gods. This means that the Old Ones do not look at a person's race or culture when they come to them, they look at the quality of the person. The members of the Odin Brotherhood I have communicated with look down on racial exclusionism. Being a blood-brother of the Gods is more important to them than the specifics of where a person hails from.'

I very much liked that. I had never been a person to evaluate people based on their race or culture. Rather, I had been raised to evaluate people on their deeds before anything else. Where some modern-day northern pagan groups followed criteria which favored Nordic or Germanic family lines, the Odin Brotherhood most certainly did not.

Crow settled back to lean against the log which was almost directly behind him. He stretched his legs out in a relaxed fashion.

'So let's discuss the nature of the Elder Ones some more, shall we?' he asked. 'And let's have a look at them from the perspective of a neo-barbarian.'

'Neo-barbarian?' I asked, images of Conan the Barbarian, a fictional creation of the late, great Robert E. Howard flashing through my mind.

'Absolutely nothing wrong with the word barbarian,' Crow retorted. 'Herd people or the masters of the herd people, people who like to think of themselves as civilized,' he made the quotation marks gesture with his hands when he said the word civilized, 'like to make barbarians out to be some kind of dirty savages but they are wrong. The Odin Brotherhood prizes the image of the barbarian because barbarians are true aspects of nature: they are free and strong. They are not corrupt.'

'They are also often instruments of balance,' I added.

'Yes!' he replied. 'And neo-barbarians are the kind of people the Odin Brotherhood seeks for its ranks. These do not all have to be great big powerful gladiator types though. It is the strength of spirit and the deep connection to the lands and the Gods that makes one a barbarian. Being fresh and clean of heart and mind can make one a barbarian: that and understanding one's place in the scheme of nature and in the sacred balance, understanding that those things which are old can be corrupt, just as our modern society is decayed and insidiously corrupt.'

'And ultimately the walls of the decayed civilizations are brought down by instruments of balance – either by nature or by the hands of barbarians,' I suggested.

'Very often that is the case,' he replied. 'You can see it in modern times actually. The world is changing; climate change, earthquakes, freakish weather happening all over the place and in the midst of this, humans are getting all the crazier. On top of this the places that were once so free are falling under heavier, oppressive governments. The Christians are losing what they once had so they are becoming more desperate to hang on to their influence in society. The Muslims are trying to spread their religion even though revolutions are happening in many of their countries. Zionists are pretty much the same as they have always been...'

'I have been told that the Odin Brotherhood does not participate in such things because these things are passing trends,' I said. 'I have been told that the Odin Brotherhood thinks in terms of centuries.'

Crow took another drink of his beer.

'I have been told that also,' he said. 'But my point is that the crazier it becomes...it is all because of corruption and decadence. The changes are already here and when they hit full-on the barbarians will play a role in tearing down the old walls: replacing them with something new and fresh.'

'We hope,' I added.

'Yes. We can only hope.'

'Wasn't it Aristotle who said, "Tolerance and Apathy are the last virtues of a dying society"?' Crow asked. 'Well, just take a look around:

that kind of behavior is everywhere. Apathy, especially, will reduce democracy to ashes in a very short time, I think.'

I found myself thinking of something an old friend of mine had once said: that we are to the Elder Kin, the Gods, as a domestic animal is to the farmer that keeps it. Like the farm animal we know of the existence of these Elder beings and we know that they have something to do with our lives but beyond that, save for the wisdom of a few who know, our perceptions of them are speculation at best and outright fantasy at worst.

I recalled also that the same person had told me he believed even the so-called cabals-of-power who supposedly manipulated the world were sadly mistaken if they thought they operated entirely under their own auspices...for indeed, the Old Ones were everywhere and often subtle in their influence.

'It's the way of nature,' Crow said. 'Everything in a huge cycle; nothing stays the same and nothing dies forever. Odin and his folk know of their fates at Ragnarök, yet they will still go to that great battle. In the end the worlds will be renewed and in the fields of Ithavöll the folk will begin again.'

We sat silently for a moment, listening to the crackle of the fire and the sound of the night around us.

'But we were talking about the Gods and the wights; the spirit people and the other Elder ones, weren't we?' he asked with a grin.

We talked for hours. In fact, the earlier fatigue I had felt slipped away in the night as we spoke. The conversation was animated and very interesting. Crow had some thoughts that I had not pondered and I had one or two things to say that he found of great interest.

In the end we could see the color of the sky begin to change. We could sense that the dawn would not be very many hours behind and we decided, at long last, to roll into our sleeping bags for sleep.

Here then is the essence of what we discussed: of the Elder Kin and their special natures.

'I can only speak from my own experience and knowledge here,'

Crow said, prefacing the earlier conversation. 'I can't speak for anyone else, the Odin Brotherhood included, because obviously I am not a member.'

I nodded at that. Crow was subtly adamant in that assertion. He wanted there to be no mistake on my part in thinking he was anything other than he was; a seeker on an Odinist path who walked a way that was in line with the ways of the Odin Brotherhood.

'Because if I was a member of the Odin Brotherhood,' he added, upon seeing my sagely nod, 'I highly doubt you and I would be here right now, talking about such stuff.'

'Why are we here then?' I asked suddenly. The question kind of slipped out of my mouth before I could properly moderate it and I was immediately silent, trying to decide whether to withdraw the question or wait for an answer. I covered with a wry smile and chose the latter.

Crow was grinning back. I suspect he had seen the sudden discomfiture behind my Cheshire grin.

'Because everyone who has taught me, from my relatives and my teachers over the years, have always told me to 'pay-it-forward' ; to pass on what I have learned. And you know, I have learned a lot...and just before I met you I was starting to realize I had not been paying forward very much.'

Pay it forward; the old adage of the late, great Robert Heinlein. I knew it well and respected that. Without passing along the things we learned – especially the profound or hard-learned lessons - great wisdom could be lost.

Crow leaned over to put another stick in the fire.

'You want to know what I think?' he asked. 'I have come a long way over the past twenty-five years as far as my paganism is concerned. I have gone from a young guy who thought of the Gods as magical beings capable of doing miracles to a guy who really sees these beings as literal genetic relations.'

I settled back against a nearby log and adjusted my feet. The cold was beginning to seep in despite the heavy insulation provided by my boots.

'I'll give you my thoughts in point form,' he said.

'One: The Gods are not really Gods in the way that most people think of Gods. They are not all knowing, all seeing people who can do magic tricks or anything like that. People have been caught up in the Judeo-Christian stuff for so many centuries they have this omnipotent-God stuff going on.'

Crow had winced comically at the last. I agreed that even in today's relatively well-educated pagan community there was a lot of the omnipotent-Gods thing going around.

'I believe they are not immortal and they can get sick, they can get hurt and they can even be killed. They don't live forever either.'

Crow finished his beer. He reached for his water bottle.

'Two: the ones you and I both agree are more Elder Kin than magical Gods are literally related to us. They are family. Extended family, maybe, but still related. I honestly believe that they made us humans or played a part in the process.'

I wholeheartedly agreed. Like Crow, I had undergone a similar evolutionary process in my development as a pagan person. For years I had suspected the Old Ones were not magical beings, but rather highly evolved, highly advanced beings who had either created us outright at some point or aided in our development as humans. I tended to favor the latter as I suspected that early primates were 'tweaked' genetically to produce an intelligent species.

'Three: They are obviously trans-dimensional, as in they can travel here from their own realm. Just more evidence of their advanced abilities,' he said. 'And because many of them have an interest in us they come here in various ways to check in and to make adjustments to things when they are needed.'

'Trans-dimensional?' I asked.

'Yes,' Crow replied. 'Trans-dimensional. The view of the Odin Brotherhood is that the Gods, as some call them, come from elsewhere but are able to step from one realm to the next by ways we Earth-bound humans can't even imagine. They come here to keep up on what's going on in Midgard.'

I thought about that for a moment. For years I had pondered the realities of the Elder Ones and what Crow had said made a lot of sense.

'Time is different for them too, as you probably know,' he added. 'It is taught in the Odin Brotherhood that time for the Gods moves at a different rate than it does here. As a matter of fact, I was told that the realm of the Old Ones exists quite literally in the past – as we think of the past. So when they visit here they are not only stepping across a bridge which brings them into our reality, they are stepping forward in time.'

'So they just step forward in time?'

'Well, they can travel anywhere they want; past, future, etc. They are not limited like us. Time has a different meaning for them.'

'You spoke of the Gods coming here to make adjustments?' I asked, referring to his earlier comment.

'Yeah,' he replied. 'Imagine if you seeded a planet with people and put a piece of yourself into them, an investment of sorts. Wouldn't you do that for a reason? And if you had a plan then wouldn't you stop by every once in awhile to make sure everything was going according to plan?'

'So the Odin Brotherhood believes the Gods are from another planet then?' I had to ask. I knew I was kind of repeating myself but I wanted clarification. I recalled something my contact had said to me once: 'The Gods are physical beings – they inhabit hidden passages in reality.' That had always deeply intrigued me.

'I don't speak for the Odin Brotherhood on that,' Crow replied. 'And I wasn't trying to suggest the Elder Ones are from another planet exactly. I was saying the Gods and Goddesses are from elsewhere, from a different place than here in Midgard. Different place, different time. I believe they are from somewhere else, yes, and they are either directly or indirectly involved in us being here, probably directly. I also believe they have plans for us.'

I had a hard time believing that the horrors which had plagued much of humanity over the last few thousand years were a part of any kind of benevolent plan. I told him that and he just smiled.

'I didn't say benevolent,' he replied. 'See, this is the thing: so many people have their heads wrapped around this Abrahamic idea that the Elder Ones are like us in those ways. Sure, they are like us in a lot of physical ways but mentally and probably even philosophically and spiritually they are a completely different ball game. People think the Gods are like us in the bad ways so they can justify doing bad things.'

Crow got up from his place and went over to the larger pile of wood he had collected. He came back with an armful and sat back down.

'I don't think that is the case at all – this thing about them being exactly like us. I don't know what their plan is either, but it's likely the plan is beyond our ability to understand right now. Look what we are doing to this rock: we are crapping all over our own den so to speak. Giving us the big picture would be like trying to explain the rules of baseball to a rat.'

'Okay, I'll play devil's advocate here,' I said. 'Why should we bother walking this road when we know we are so far below the Elder Kin we can't possibly comprehend them?'

Crow laughed and spread his hands in a wide open gesture.

'See, that's the thing,' he said, looking at me with an expression that said *'I know you get this!'* 'Most people have no idea about what the Gods are really about. They have so much of their childhood programming left that they can't – or don't want – to believe the Gods are anything other than their fantasy versions of them. They are herd animals in a lot of ways...even many pagans are content to just eat up grass and settle for being church-goers disguised as something else.' The hands came down but the expression remained on Crow's face.

'Now seekers on the path of the Odin Brotherhood are a very different animal entirely,' he continued. 'They are willing and able to look past all of the crap that has piled up in the conscious experience of most of humanity. They are willing to look past it and to take that mental and spiritual leap which tells them one important thing.'

'And what might that be?' I asked. I already knew the answer but I wanted to hear it from the Crow's mouth, so to speak.

'That thing, as you well know, is that the Gods notice the farmyard humans who have woken up, or at least those of us who are in the process of doing that. I think...and I am not the only one...that the Elder Ones notice it when people like us wake up and when that happens they take an interest in that person. I honestly believe that is the underlying current in the whole belief system of the Odin Brotherhood.'

'When people awaken the Gods take notice, and when they notice they take interest. Interest leads to contact,' I said.

'Bingo!' he said.

'The belief is that the Gods are real beings who take an interest in our world, and in those of us who are genetically related to them. They understand that most humans are still dumb animals who think mainly about sex or eating or in finding ways to be comfortable, but they also know there are some who are waking up; people who would understand and learn from direct contact if it happened.'

'And, playing the advocate again here,' I said, 'what do those of us who are awakened get out of direct contact?'

'What did you get when your dad took you fishing or when you had time to spend with your grandfather?' he asked. 'Wisdom and knowledge, buddy, which is really what it is all about; learning and moving forward are the keys here. That's the plan we were talking about.'

I knew where he was going with this line of thought. I agreed with him. The greater part of humanity was doing a pretty terrific job of transforming themselves into a more efficient form of herd animal and the Earth was suffering grievously as the number of ever-consuming humans grew day by day. Slowly but surely however – perhaps it was a side effect of increased access to information via the internet, or perhaps more effective methods of education – there were people who were waking up. The modern-day revival of various pagan religions and cultural spiritualities was evidence of this.

In my own case the gradual awakening had taken years as I fought my way clear, first, of my Protestant Christian upbringing and then, later, as I sorted through all of the options that were available to the spiritual seeker out there. For me it was a time of adventure but also a time of sometimes great confusion as I had to rebuild what should have been my birthright beneath the almost constant mainstream messages demanding that I conform, dumb down and just 'fit in,' 'don't rock the boat,' or just 'be normal.'

I had never been like that, however; a conformist. I had never been normal. My journey had, at times, been like struggling up a steep hill covered with thorn bushes and other harsh obstacles. At times it felt as though the very universe was trying to push me back down; back into the comfortable embrace of a population I had never really been a part of to begin with.

I knew that Crow had felt that way and had experienced similar things. We had a few conversations about that and he had specifically requested that they be 'off the record' – in other words, not recorded for use in the book. I respected this because I too knew where he was coming from on a good number of issues and in some ways I had experienced some of the rough roads that he had.

'We need to learn and move forward because the Gods have seen what we are doing to this planet and they are trying to help us along to head off disaster,' Crow said suddenly. 'They are here often and I am sure they see it firsthand. The madness will have to be reined in.'

I nodded from my place at the fire. I agreed with what he said. The world was spinning out of control – had been spinning out of control for a long time now. The insanity of a world rushing headlong toward its own annihilation had to be brought to an end.

'The Gods visit here, you know,' Crow said.

He had said that before to me; several times since I had known him.

'Have you ever met one?' I asked. I was curious and as I asked the question I could feel the slight tingle of excitement run up my spine – for I would have bet money on his answer.

'Yes,' he said. 'I'm sure of it. One night out on the road a visitor stopped by where I was camping. He asked me a few questions, just mundane things, but I could feel it in his presence. Before I knew it he was gone back into the night, just like that.'

I had experienced something similar, years ago, when I had been visiting an archeological site in southern Alberta. I had been standing at a cliffside admiring the sweeping prairie when I noticed the black shadow of a massive thunderstorm approaching from the southeast. A very large, bearded man with a heavy German accent suddenly appeared next to me. I had not seen him approach and it momentarily startled me. We exchanged one or two mundane words concerning the landscape and the weather. He seemed keenly interested in me and what I had to say. It was almost unnerving, to be honest, but I kept my feelings to myself and remained polite. Finally, he commented on the approaching storm and made the analogy that there was a storm approaching mankind as well – and that it would be wise for people like me to go *looking to find my kin and my people.*

At the time what he said had not seemed to make any sense to me, but I nodded politely at his comment. He bade me farewell and left the area shortly after that. I never saw him again, but the feeling that he was something other than the common man has stayed in my memory for many years since then.

It is said that when one is called to consider the Sojourn of the

Brave, drawn to the initiation rite of the Brotherhood, it begins with a potent dream. There are many who believe such dreams are the acts of Elder Ones who speak to their chosen ones through such dreams.

I took a moment and told Crow the tale of the bearded visitor and after a moment he said, 'Yep. Sounds like one of them. You can feel it somehow. It is not something you can really describe. Other than the stranger's eyes, that is. They were very, very dark. It was like if you looked at them too long you could get lost in his gaze, yet on the other hand in his company I felt like I was with a big brother who would never let anything bad get near me.'

There was a brief moment of deep silence as I pondered his words. I could also tell by the tone of his voice – something I cannot convey in the written word - that he was speaking from a very deeply emotional place in his heart.

'It felt like he was family, unconditionally. No fear. Only kinship,' Crow said after a moment. 'And after he was gone I felt a hole there in my space that I think has been there ever since. It's like a brother goes off to war or something and you never see him again.'

I knew exactly what he was speaking of. The Odin Brotherhood tells that often one might note the presence of a visiting God or Goddess if one finds themselves in the presence of someone who is extraordinarily beautiful or handsome in appearance, or who exudes an uncommonly strong aura or charisma. It is also said that often those who are among the Elder Ones cast no shadows while visiting Midgard. I can attest to the feeling of presence while in the proximity of someone like that, though at the time I made no note of things like shadows.

'It's not always like that,' Crow said mildly. 'Direct contact is not as common as I make it sound, though it is getting more frequent. For the most part the Elder Ones are pretty good at keeping their presence a secret and a lot of the ways they communicate with us humans is through a network of spies and informants.'

'Spies and informants?'

'Makes sense doesn't it?' he asked. 'Most humans are not ready for a physical experience with one of their makers. In fact most people are probably happy in their ignorance. No, it is better at this stage in the game to use messengers and spies to get the idea across. I have no doubt that many of the Gods are doing this. At least the ones who give a rat's ass about the survival of their folk.'

I knew where he was going with that too. We had at another point discussed the theory of what a teacher of mine had referred to as God-Tribes. If Midgard was seeded by Elder beings, human beings of differing ethno-cultural origins may have been made by a kind of patron/patroness God or Goddess; there may be 'races' of Elder Kin who reflect their own heritage through the humans who were placed by them on Midgard. Thus it is believed by some that Asian people, for instance, were placed by Elders who were also of that physical type and that Asian people would be watched over and tutored over time by their own sets of Elder Kin. The same would apply to Africans and those of India, northern and central Europe, etc.

Crow's comment reflected the apparent disparity between the beliefs of some religious/cultural groups and their actual actions on the Earth. He believed that like us humans, the Elder Ones were all different and have differing personalities and behaviors. He was of the opinion that the God of the Abrahamic religions, for instance, known by some as Jehovah, had caused much damage to the world by instilling in his followers a sense of ownership and self-entitlement over the resources and peoples of the Earth.

'Messengers might be anybody,' Crow continued. 'They might be someone who writes a book or an internet blog. They might be someone you meet in a coffee shop or something like that. The idea is that they are like us. They know, and they are trying to get the message out in a subtle way – to wake up a few more people up if they can. Sometimes they communicate directly, sometimes they use technology like letters or the internet. I have been told that members of the Odin Brotherhood also use books in libraries as the means to convey information.'

I had heard that one myself: that at certain times mysterious packets of information, sometimes something as simple as a sheet of paper tucked between the pages of a volume, might be the way that information about the Brotherhood or other matters was conveyed. The Odin Brotherhood had many such ways of getting their ideas and messages across.

'The idea is that the more of us who are awake, the better chance that the disaster we are heading into can be stopped. And once it is stopped we can concentrate on moving forward as a species.'

It was my turn to go and fetch more firewood. I noticed the moment I got up how our small fire had created a globe of warmth and cheer around us, and when I left that globe I immediately noticed how brittle cold the mountain air had become. I quickly gathered up a pile of wood, thankful we had the foresight to collect it all earlier in the day, and made my way back to my spot.

'Contacts are becoming more frequent. You know that, don't you?' Crow asked from across the fire. It leaped and sparked a little as I added a piece of wood.

'Yes,' I replied. Again I was not sure if it was the advent of the internet, but as people communicated more clearly and often, more and more tales of people having encounters with mysterious people had made their way to me. Indeed mysterious encounters of all kinds seemed to be increasing; from numerous reports of crop circles to unidentified flying objects, even to encounters of what some might term paranormal, had apparently been increasing worldwide.

'The veil between worlds is getting thinner,' Crow said. 'I don't think it will be too many more years now until there is a reckoning for the last two thousand years of darkness and I think that is yet another reason why the Odin Brotherhood has made itself known.'

'Agents of balance?' I asked.

'Could be part of it,' he said. 'The reawakening has begun and all over the planet people are waking up and asking, "What have these religions and government guys done to our planet?"'

'The Gods are walking Midgard more and more these days,' Crow continued. 'Some of them anyway, those who take an active interest. They want to protect their people, their younger kin. They want to wake up those who can be awakened and help them to fight for their rightful place in Midgard once again.'

Our conversation turned, after a few moments, to the mundane. We spoke awhile about camping and fishing and several other outdoor activities. After awhile Crow suddenly yawned and stood up.

'I am bagged. Gonna hit the sack.' And with that he headed to where his small tent was set up in the shadow of an old, wizened pine tree.

After a few moments all was quiet again and I spent the next half hour or so pondering the things we had spoken about during the evening. Finally I doused the remains of the fire and crawled into my own little tent and sleeping bag. I expected to lie awake for some time thinking, but that was not to be the case. Within mere moments the fresh air and other factors had their way and I fell into a deep, satisfied slumber.

5

Lore of the Shrouded

The mobile phone rang insistently in my pocket. I was standing in a crowded bus heading out to the university. At first I thought I would simply let it go to message, but I thought better of it.

'It's been awhile,' said the familiar voice on the line.

'About two months,' I replied. 'Thanks for the beer, by the way.'

It had indeed been some two months since I had last seen the enigmatic fellow I knew as Crow. The last instance had been in a tiny campsite in the trees above the small city of Squamish and we had spoken long into the night about the nature of things.

I had emerged from my tent the next morning to discover that Crow had left the camp early in the hours of dawn. He left me with a bottle of beer accompanied by a note on a small piece of paper that said: 'Wisdom earnestly traded last night, bro. Thanks!'

I had made my way back to the city on my own. I had not seen or heard from him since that time.

'You sound like you are on a bus,' he said in an amused tone.

I informed him that indeed I was on a bus. I was heading to the library at the university to do some research.

'Well, if you want to see something interesting, jump off that bus and get on another one,' he said, suddenly all business. The call did not last much longer than that. He gave me a downtown location and a time to meet. That was all.

I grudgingly got off the bus I had been traveling on and switched to one that was bound in the opposite direction. I was somewhat irritated at Crow's habit of disappearing for long periods of time and then popping up unexpectedly, usually then to throw my schedule off as I dropped everything to accommodate him. Still, he had not disappointed me to date, and there was no doubt in my mind he knew a lot more about our mutual interest, the Odin Brotherhood, than I did.

I disembarked from the bus into the wet streets of the area known as the Downtown Eastside. There had been an afternoon rain and even though it had long passed much of the wetness remained in the streets. The Downtown Eastside is not a pretty place and though I had been there many times in the past, it was never really an area of town I enjoyed venturing into – especially not as nighttime approached.

I walked along the damp sidewalk for several minutes,

occasionally looking for the cross street that Crow had directed me towards. The quality of the area got gradually worse and before long I was making my way down a side street populated mostly by homeless people, prostitutes and their customers. This was not a safe area even in the light of midday; it was a home for gangs and drug dealers and worse, and though I could well take care of myself in an altercation, I had no interest in getting myself into trouble of any kind.

I moved into an area with which I was well familiar. It was roughly the same area where, years ago, I had been working on the commercial video project and had, while in the dank basement of an old building, seen the Eye of Odin painted in deep blue upon an old brick wall.

A creepy sensation tingled up my spine as I walked past the entrance to that old ramshackle building. I was very relieved – or rather my nose was - that I did not see Crow anywhere about. I had little interest in once again descending into the filthy warrens I knew to lurk on the floors beneath.

Finally I saw him standing against a light post in a dark grey overcoat and brimmed hat, looking every bit like he had emerged from the cover of some old detective novel. He waved me over to where he was and after we shook hands he started down a nearby laneway.

'Follow me,' he said.

We traveled down the lane to the end and then took a left. There, across the street, was a really old red brick and concrete structure. Probably the building had been quite handsome when it had been new, back in the early 20th century. Now it was run-down and falling apart. The windows and doors of the lower floor had been boarded up and there were city notices pasted across the doorway. It looked as though the old building had come to the end of the line.

'It will be demolished soon,' Crow confirmed as he ducked down a very narrow laneway at the side of the building. 'Someone told me about this place just the other day and I thought you might like to see this before the demolition guys come in here.'

I simply nodded and followed him. As I say, this is a rough neighborhood. I thought it best not to be caught loitering around by either police or gangs.

Crow stopped about halfway down the length of the lane and pulled on a very narrow metal door set into the wall. It opened. I was surprised because usually when the city plans on demolishing a structure they go to great pains to seal it off so it will not become a habitation for homeless people – or worse; a crack house or the like. Yet the door swung open for Crow as if he possessed a key. I had not seen him use one in the lock panel on the door, yet I would not have put it past him.

Inside he handed me a small flashlight, which, when I clicked it on, had an unusually bright beam.

'We go up to the top,' he said gesturing to the old, worn wooden steps in front of us.

He closed the door to the laneway, which clicked with the sound of a lock engaging. It seemed ominous and loud in the cavernous dark of the stairwell.

Crow took the lead and began to climb. As I followed I wondered if this building had been constructed before the advent of the elevator. I doubted it, and surmised that if there had been an elevator in the structure it would probably be more toward the front of the building. Either way, as the entire place was without power, the lift would have been useless to us in any case. I pondered though the efforts that people in the past must have had to put in when moving things like furniture and such up numerous flights of narrow stairs.

The building was nine stories high. My legs were well aware of that, too, as we finally emerged on the landing and Crow stopped for a brief rest.

'This building was once pretty impressive I bet,' he said from the gloom ahead of me. 'Did you notice the place does not reek like so many others in this part of town do?'

I had noticed that. The place smelled of old wood and slightly, of mold, but missing were things like the smell of rotting garbage or urine, hallmarks often found in old buildings in neighborhoods like this one.

'I think the owners took care of the place,' Crow said. 'They were careful to keep it locked to certain types of people. I was told that it held offices and things like that right up till the end.'

'I wonder what kind of offices in this day and age?' I pondered out loud.

The building looked quite antiquated on many levels and even the electrical outlets I had seen in the walls looked as though they had not been modernized in any way. I had difficulty believing that the needs of a modern-day business office could be accommodated in an aging edifice such as this.

'I was surprised that some developer didn't try to renovate it into luxury condos or something,' Crow said as he started toward the 9th floor access.

'In this hood?' I asked incredulously. Indeed, the city had seen the widespread gentrification of many areas which had formerly been run-down, but this area in particular would have some years to wait as far as I was concerned.

We moved through the heavy wooden door and into a short hallway beyond. I wondered about the short hallway as it served no appreciable purpose. This short passage ended in a solid wooden door with a worn, brass knob. Crow pushed it inward and it swung silently open, revealing a much longer hall that had office-style doorways along it on each side. The doors looked to be made of some kind of old hardwood and had large, frosted glass windows in them about halfway up. Interestingly, none of the doors had markings on them of any kind as one might expect to see. Normally one would expect at least a suite number or the name of the business or occupant marked on the door or on the window.

The hallway was, of course, quite dark. Most of the windows had been boarded up on the lower floors and on the upper ones there was little light getting in to the hallway. Had we not possessed the flashlights our adventure would have borne little fruit.

Crow walked along the hall directly to the door set into the end of the passage. It was exactly the same as all of the others with no markings of any kind. He paused only a moment before opening it and gesturing me inside.

Once inside I realized we were in some kind of waiting room. It was small but there was still an old wooden desk there and a heavy wooden bookshelf built into the wall. It also seemed to have once held a couch and several chairs (there were markings on the old, off-white linoleum-covered floor) though those had been removed.

Behind the desk, off to one side and set into the wall, was a large, double door. It was not particularly ornate, but still it looked rather grand compared with the small, rather spare-looking entry area. Crow took the handle of one half of the door and opened it inwards. I followed.

In a moment I realized we were in a large room that for a change had unblocked windows. The windows were grimy and dimmed with dust, most of it outside, yet they let in considerably more light than had been in any other part of the building I had seen. The room had a high ceiling and the floor appeared to be made of well-polished wood of some kind. The room was somewhat square in shape and had large, expansive bookshelves set deeply into the walls. The bookshelves, like the rest of the room, were completely empty.

'Move to the center of the room,' Crow suggested, and so I did that. In the dim light of the room I could make out his face and I could see he had a mischievous semi-grin.

'Look down,' he said.

I did as I was asked and within a second I felt a familiar chill run down my spine. For there, in a circular section of tile set into the wood, was a symbol I had seen before. The setting was circular, about the same diameter as a trash-can lid. It had been set flush with the surface of the wooden floor.

Before me was a depiction, deep blue on crimson, of a single eye. The circle was enclosed by a ring of worn, gold tile about an inch wide that had symbols I could not identify in the dim light. Even under the flashlight beam they were so worn, probably by years of being walked over, that I could not make them out. The glyph was a rendition of the same Eye of Odin symbol I had seen years earlier in the sub-basement of a decaying tenement building not far away.

The Eye was rounded and elongated, perhaps somewhat like the ancient Egyptian Eye of Ra but far simpler in depiction. The tile-setter had done a magnificent job in tiny square ceramic bits that made the glyph look almost as if it had been painted on the crimson-red background by a brush rather than otherwise.

'How did you find out about this place?' I asked, my voice barely above a whisper. I was trying to come to a conclusion in my mind as to how the exact same symbol had found its way from a crumbling basement off skid row to a finely-crafted tile setting in what was obviously once a well-to-do office building.

'I have my sources,' he said.

'I bet you do,' I replied. 'Can you read the script around the outside?'

'No,' he replied. 'But I believe I have seen something like it before. It looks suspiciously runic.'

The tile symbol below my feet was very old. It was worn and scuffed and from the looks of the floor surface it had spent some years concealed by a large area rug. Yet the work itself was very fine – just like the wood paneling and other work in the room. I suspected the tile setting had been there since the construction of the building many years earlier. Someone – or some 'ones' of importance had once used this place, I was certain.

'Take a good look, man,' Crow said. 'Because it is the last time either of us will ever see this room again.'

I thought about the boarded-up windows and the notices plastered on the building. Yes, the building would not have many hours left in the world of men.

My mind leapt forward in a rush of ideas. I thought of coming back with a saw, or at least bringing a camera so the image could be preserved.

'I was told not to try to remove the symbol or take any pictures,' Crow said suddenly, as if gleaning my thoughts. He grinned briefly at the look of surprise that must have painted itself across my face.

'It is not their way, nor should it be ours,' he added. 'The lore is spread differently.'

Suddenly a very loud crash sounded from somewhere on the lower floors of the building. It sounded almost like a gunshot followed by a larger noise – perhaps that of something large falling over.

Both of us froze, but only for a moment before we took our leave of the room as quickly as we could. Whatever mysteries this place held would have to remain with the ghosts of its past.

We made our way down the hallway to the stairs and there on the landing we listened intently. There was another loud sound that echoed briefly and then was silent. It sounded again as though something heavy had been pushed over.

'Sounds like it is coming from the front of the building,' Crow said quietly. 'We had better leave.'

And so we did, making our way down the flights of stairs and finally, without any trouble, through the metal door and back into the now-darkened laneway.

We walked along to the lane's entrance and from there traveled away along the sidewalk. The cause of the noise was explained to us as we saw the plywood had been torn off one of the old entry doors. No doubt some locals had decided to go exploring inside.

No one noticed us as we made our way out of the area.

* * *

'Slainte!' Crow said, hoisting his glass and drinking.

I returned the toast and took a sip of the dark brew in my glass. Guinness; long a favorite of mine. This was especially true when it was served in the little Irish pub not far from campus that had for many years been a special place for me.

It had started to rain within a few moments of our leaving the condemned building and to expedite our departure from the neighborhood we had hailed a cab. Half an hour later found us seated in a comfortable spot near the back of the aforementioned pub, burgers in front of us and frosty beverages at hand.

Little had been said about the experience in the old building once we had left it, and the ride in the cab had been filled with mundane pleasantries. However, once we had settled into the comforting dimness of the pub, our conversation turned to the mystery at hand.

'Someone I know suggested I might have a look at something which was soon to be lost to the memory of this city,' Crow said enigmatically in explanation of his source. 'I went in there yesterday evening and when I saw what I saw I thought right away about you.'

'Me and my little quest, eh?' I asked.

'Yes,' he said. 'I get the impression you have seen that symbol before.'

'I have,' I said. 'Twice now.' And I proceeded to tell him about my experience years earlier in the sub-basement of that downtrodden structure.

Crow nodded in a sagely fashion once I had finished speaking. 'Exactly the same symbol?' he asked.

'The eye was exactly the same symbol,' I replied. 'Right down to the color of the glyph. The crimson-colored background and the inscription around it I have not seen before but I am positive it was exactly the same as I remember.'

'I have seen this symbol before as well,' he said. 'Three times before.'

I took a sip of my Guinness. It was cool and flavorful. I was finally relaxing, glad to be away from that run-down neighborhood — not so much because I was concerned for my safety, but because I always felt a deep sadness when I walked those streets. What was once a very happy, prosperity-filled place had been reduced to despair and squalor that fairly radiated from the walls. It was difficult not to be affected by that.

Having said that I was equally glad we had not had any run-ins with the local gang culture down there. It would likely not have been pleasant.

'You saw the same symbol as the one set in the floor?' I asked, becoming more and more intrigued.

'Never in tile like that,' Crow replied, 'But once in paint on a wall, like you saw. Another time on a piece of paper hidden in a book.'

'And the other time?' I inquired.

Crow was suddenly silent. It was as if he was mulling over something in his head and trying rapidly to decide if he should tell me or not.

Finally he relented with a slight smile. 'The second time was in blue ink, on a person's right inner forearm,' he said. 'But don't ask any more right now because I won't say anything more on that subject.'

'Fair enough,' I said. 'But what do you think is the significance of the glyph?'

'It's pretty obvious to me,' he replied. 'It's the Eye of Odin. It doesn't just look like it to me...it feels like it too. Blue has been associated with Odin as well so the color matches.'

I had my own theories. The main one was that there was an

underground resurgence of pagan or even Odinist thought taking place in urban areas and that many, including the people of the streets, were gradually finding their way back. My old friend and teacher Ari had told me to watch for signs of what he had termed the 're-awakening' in the opening decades of the 21st century, and more and more the things I had seen were proving his vision to be true.

I imagined that Crow had a similar theory since from our conversations I had come to know that we thought alike on many levels. I had little doubt that one of the reasons he had shown me the old building was because it confirmed yet another part of that commonly held theory.

'I believe the symbol may be a sign of the Odin Brotherhood,' Crow said finally.

His comment caught me off guard. I set my glass down carefully and stared at him.

'Are you serious?' I asked.

I had never heard of the Odin Brotherhood having a symbol before, though I had long suspected they might. I had made inquiries to that effect, actually, through my contacts and other means, but my requests for clarification had always been met with ambiguous responses. No one had ever told me that *'No, there was certainly no actual symbol,'* however they had never admitted to one either. I had been told that with the Odin Brotherhood it was the quest that mattered, not necessarily the possession. Perhaps that also applied to symbology though I found it difficult to fathom.

I was reminded of something I had been told not that long ago by a contact: *'We use mystery to inspire thought.'*

'Yeah, I am serious,' Crow replied. 'There are too many things that line up with that train of thought. I think there are some things that can only be known from within the Brotherhood and the rest are kind of like breadcrumbs that people like you and I get that might lead us to the source.'

'It is an interesting thought,' I said, pondering what he had said.

'If they have icons, talismans and mysterious idols, why can't the Brotherhood have a secret symbol?' Crow said suddenly. He half whispered the last part of the sentence as if he had not intended to say what he had said.

I froze.

'What icons, talismans and mysterious idols?' I asked with deep interest.

Crow immediately got that look on his face: one I had already in a short time become familiar with. It was the sudden closed-doors-behind-the-eyes look that told me he did not want to tell me more at the time.

He held up his glass.

'Too much sauce for the goose?' he asked, the familiar grin returning to his face.

'You are not going to say anything else on the subject right now, are you?' I asked. I was frustrated and I could not figure out his reasoning. I had never before heard of mysterious idols or any other such thing from any of my reading or contacts. I wanted to know more but I found myself facing a roadblock.

'Didn't say never, bro,' he said finally. 'But I will need to think on that for a bit.'

'You are as difficult to get information out of as the Odin Brotherhood,' I stated flatly.

'Who knows?' Crow said finally, diverting the subject. 'I have found that the best way to get information from the Odin Brotherhood is to put your query out there by various means and wait for them to contact you. I have been told several times by them that for the most part they prefer to communicate in one-of-a-kind manifestations for most people. That way they continue their traditions of mystery.'

'But they don't do that with everyone,' I added.

'No, obviously not,' he replied. 'We are both examples of that.'

'Physical drop boxes, back channels, e-mail "dead-drops,"

encrypted forums, mysterious phone calls and even more mysterious people appearing out of nowhere...this is the world of the Odin Brotherhood, my friend,' Crow added. 'As they have told me, they are few but they are everywhere. This is how they are slowly creating change in Midgard. They are far more powerful than anyone imagines and they have their resources and ways to do what needs to be done.'

'Sounds like a plot for a James Bond movie,' I said.

'But far cooler,' he replied.

I gave up on the subject of the mysterious idols for the time being. I already knew Crow well enough to know that if he wanted to tell me something he would do so on his own time. I would wait.

We sat there for a moment in silence, each with his thoughts and enjoying the food and drink that was in front of us.

'Thanks for showing me that room in the old building,' I said. 'It was very interesting and I know you went out of your way to do that.'

'It was nothing, besides I wanted to have one more look myself.'

'The Odin Brotherhood, if indeed it was their people who placed that symbol there, work in strange and mysterious ways.'

'They like it that way,' Crow replied.

Again silence descended. The pub was quiet and we had most of the rear of the establishment to ourselves. Other than the occasional sounds of two Englishmen arguing good naturedly about politics up at the bar, the place was almost completely silent - other than the minute sounds we made as we ate.

'Probably now would be a good time to talk about the customs of the Odin Brotherhood,' Crow said, finishing off his pint. 'I figure since we were talking about their tendency to be mysterious and all, well, maybe we can compare notes.'

I was game for that. I told him right then and there however, that I doubted anything I could reveal would be news to him.

He just grinned and ordered another pint from the ever- attentive server, who seemed to have an instinct for when a customer desired another pint.

As we did not want our discussion intruded upon we waited a few minutes until the young lady returned with his beverage.

'Something about Guinness,' he said, toasting me. 'It's a very smooth and comforting brew. I try not to drink too many of them.'

I agreed with this sentiment. Like the Irish who invented it, Guinness was a subtle yet potent concoction. As with any alcoholic drink it was unwise to have too many.

'The way to the Odin Brotherhood is twofold I think,' Crow began. 'I think most people hear of the Brotherhood first in some way. Later, if it is their destiny, they have a powerful dream that tells them to look for more.'

That was the version of things that I agreed with. This was fairly common knowledge.

'I came into contact with the idea of the Odin Brotherhood through a library book, believe it or not,' he said. 'I was doing research on something somewhat unrelated and there folded into the back part of the book was a piece of paper. The paper gave a few brief details about a mysterious secret society known only as the Odin Brotherhood.'

'Very interesting,' I said. I had heard of this method before. There were rumors that the Odin Brotherhood would insert literature into books in libraries in the hope that if the right person happened upon it, they might seek to know more. My own introduction had come through a mentor, but any manner of discovering the keys to new knowledge was fine in my books – rather ingenious too, I thought.

'What was the book you were reading?' I asked curiously.

'Nietzsche,' he said. 'I was taking a class in philosophy at the time. Finding the piece of paper was totally unexpected.'

It was not an extreme stretch of the imagination that an agent of the Odin Brotherhood might secret a small flyer of some kind in such a book.

'Well, it was a book concerning Germanic culture in a way,' I said. 'Not such a stretch perhaps?'

'Maybe I should go see if there are any interesting notes in the Sigmund Freud books?' He grinned.

I grinned back. Maybe that was not such a stretch either, but I rather doubted it.

'At the time I had never even heard of the Odin Brotherhood,' he continued. 'This was some time back, mind you, and while I had been a pagan for years and had tried – and discarded the modern versions of the Old Ways - I found myself instantly intrigued by this simple little piece of paper. I tried to force myself to read the chapters of the book on Nietzsche, but at the time I couldn't do it; that little piece of paper kept calling me back. So finally I gave in, pulled up to a computer and started investigating.'

'And you found Mark Mirabello's book,' I suggested the next step.

'Yes, ordering a copy of that book was the next step,' he replied. 'Though while I was waiting I did a fair bit of looking around on the internet. After awhile I gave up on that though because the idiot-to-normal ratio on the subject was way too high. I know in retrospect now that probably half of everybody who has read the book think it's a hoax, a quarter think it's true but look no further and the final twenty-five percent go around thinking that it's some kind of Satanic cult. Even among the so-called heathens it seems to be a similar split.'

'Sounds like the way most people are on the internet about a lot of things,' I said.

'Lots of crackpots out there, my friend,' Crow concluded.

I pointed out that we were getting sidetracked. He laughed good naturedly and agreed.

'A contact I have later found my surprise at finding an Odin Brotherhood flyer in a textbook amusing,' he said. 'I was told that many such techniques are employed by the Brotherhood. It was all about spreading the lore around so that in the event of a return to a Dark Age the Old Ways would be preserved.'

I too had heard something to that extent. I had been told that sometimes, to certain people, mysterious letters, unsigned and with no return address, would be sent. At other times packages would arrive. Sometimes, I had been informed, telephone calls would be made to people who the Brotherhood found of interest. In these ways the Odin Brotherhood would spread the knowledge of their existence and possibly pique the interest of a few.

'Did you know that in the old days there was even the custom of placing literature in a bottle, sealing it, and tossing it into the ocean?' Crow asked. He was smiling brightly and I could tell he thought that was a very cool idea.

I had never heard that one. I told him so.

'It is a very interesting method of getting information out there,' he said. 'Long John Silver style.'

The tradition of secreting information was something I had only been familiar with for a few months before I met Crow, yet my old mentors Max and Werner, in particular, had suspected such things. Finally I had asked bluntly and my contact had told me about the various methods of spreading the lore. I was told that it was not at all uncommon for members to hide copies of Odin Brotherhood literature in various places. These would be placed in libraries, or in bookstores and other repositories of knowledge. Sometimes these things would be hidden in different locations. This practice had, I was told, been going on for centuries and that in many cases it might sit for anywhere from a few years to a few hundred years before they were discovered.

'Nowadays they use the internet as well,' Crow said. 'There is a lot of garbage to wade through but I am certain they have people who are quite expert at using that medium.'

I didn't blame them for that. Even though I knew the Odin Brotherhood to be a tradition that was safeguarded by a layered, cellular structure, I also knew that it always paid to be safe rather than sorry. The Odin Brotherhood was very open and transparent about its lore, but the membership was always a very secure secret. I had the impression that one needed to earn the trust of those who might one day contact them and in the confusion of the internet this was not always so simple to achieve.

I told Crow this and he agreed that it was wise to remain in the shadows, ever watchful and guarded, for the dark times were upon the world once – they could be again.

'The Odin Brotherhood was nearly wiped out once, did you know that?'

I told him that no, I had not heard that. I was not surprised though, considering all the attempts of literal genocide that had been attempted on tribal pagan people all over the world. I suspected a tradition like the Odin Brotherhood would have been perceived as a substantial threat in various times and places throughout history.

'Yes,' Crow said. 'From what I was told it was a close one, too. Apparently there was one single family in Europe somewhere, that at one time was the last remaining island of the Odin Brotherhood ways. Lucky for us they survived.'

I requested details on this near-miss event but Crow admitted that he had little else to add.

'My contact was hesitant to say much more so I didn't push him on the matter,' he said. 'I assume that the agents of the church at the time may have been responsible or maybe for other reasons the lore had not been properly spread around.'

In the old days the tradition of the Odin Brotherhood was something that was passed from person to person over large spans of time. Often, I imagined, the lore would be spread within families and to close friends and associates. It was not as it is in today's world of mass media and the internet: one had to be excruciatingly careful about trusting anyone with such knowledge.

Modern-day people, many of whom criticize secret orders and

demand transparency in everything, have little comprehension of the horrors that faced pagan people in ages past. They do not understand that certain things are designed to be held by few, not many and they do not understand that in circular or spherical time what has been before will be again. The Odin Brotherhood has not survived six centuries by being open and transparent.

'The Odin Brotherhood does not believe in the concept of equality,' Crow said suddenly. I could tell he had been having similar thoughts to my own. 'The Odin Brotherhood looks to nature for guidance and in nature there is stratification. Some people are not desired as friends of the Gods. Others are. It's that simple and it's why someone I know told me that for every hundred people who may be interested in the Brotherhood, perhaps a few might be worthy...perhaps.'

'I suspect that the Odin Brotherhood, through its network of agents and spies, watches certain people to see if they are of sufficient interest to warrant contacting,' I suggested.

'That is highly likely,' Crow responded. 'The placement of literature out in various locations is considered a way of perhaps interesting those worthy few in finding out more. Once people who are interested make themselves known they are probably watched for awhile to see if they are worth communicating with.'

'And once someone is found who might be worthy of communicating with they are offered ways of finding out more about the Brotherhood,' I said.

'Correct,' Crow said. 'You and I are examples of such contacts. But did you know that there are some interesting ways in which the Odin Brotherhood has helped certain people along on their paths of discovery? I was told of one in which a person of interest would be sent a sum of cash or other valued form of trade. The gift would have a map included with it that led to another location. The second location would also contain a similar gift with yet another map leading to a third location. The third location would contain Odin Brotherhood literature along with a message.'

I leaned forward slightly in anticipation and I asked what the message was.

'Use the money and the knowledge to achieve greatness. When you have achieved greatness, spread the money and the knowledge,' he said.

I leaned back in my seat. 'Nice,' I said. 'That would certainly get someone's attention.'

'Yes it would,' Crow commented. 'Sometimes in certain circumstances a person of interest to them may even get invited to mysterious dinners at exotic locations, as Dr. Mirabello did. I believe they chose him because they knew that he would be a good person to carry a piece of their message out into the world.'

I had no doubt of that. Dr. Mirabello's book had spread quite well around the world following its publication. Many who had not known of the Odin Brotherhood or their philosophy had been given access to it through the book.

'He is not a member of the Odin Brotherhood,' Crow said. He had said this to me before on more than one occasion now.

'I know that,' I replied. 'No doubt they make use of people who they think may help them to spread knowledge.'

'And who better than a historian with an open mind?' Crow asked.

I had to agree with that. There were no doubt many who were somehow associated, however peripherally, with the Odin Brotherhood who were not actual members. Some had simply agreed to help spread the knowledge of the Brotherhood's existence. Others had directly helped spread the lore. I believed that the actual percentage of people who were initiates was much lower.

'So, when a person is deemed sufficiently interesting they are contacted,' I said. 'This contact can take various forms and can range from once or twice in a lifetime for a particular person, to more continual communications for others. The contacts can be anything from mysterious letters or e-mails, to packages, phone calls or even face-to-face meetings.'

'Yep,' Crow said. 'It's kind of like a fork in the trail too, I think. Not everyone is cut out to walk the ways of the Odin Brotherhood. It can be a lonely existence for some and possibly too much to bear for others. It's often at this point when people decide whether they would like to initiate or to simply be of use in the spread of the lore.'

Indeed the tradition of the Brotherhood tells us that in order to initiate one must first be called by a dream or a vision leading them to initiate into the Brotherhood. Not all will have such dreams; some will walk only that far and no further. Some, however, will choose to go all the way and seek initiation.

'The unworthy exclude themselves,' Crow said rather sternly. A momentary shadow glazed his face and then, as quickly as it had descended upon him, it passed and his rounded face rebounded back to its much more characteristic Han Solo-esque half grin.

'The Brotherhood demands much from its members and promises nothing in return. Such conditions attract the great and repel all who are small, cowardly and smug.'

'That sounds familiar,' I said.

'It is a direct quote from 'ol Doc Mirabello's book as a matter of fact, so credit given,' Crow smiled. 'It's true, too. And I will tell you this, too,' Crow said. 'Someone told me that the Odin Brotherhood realistically looks at their efforts as being long term but also a long shot. I was told that among humans only 4% are leaders; only 4% are of interest to those-who-know. The rest are followers, parasites or scoundrels.'

My contact had told me several stories in which selected people had been chosen to participate in face-to-face meetings with members of the Brotherhood. It was said that in light of the fact that one of the goals of the Odin Brotherhood was to become friends with the Gods, there were times when actual Gods or Goddesses would be present at such meetings. If such a thing were indeed true then the opportunity to attend such gatherings would be quite rare and special.

'The Elder Ones have appeared at Odin Brotherhood gatherings,' Crow commented momentarily. 'I have even heard that there are people out there, right in our age, who have been given apples.'

'Do you mean Idun's apples?' I asked in surprised awe. 'The fruit of youth?'

The evening was getting better and better as far as I was concerned.

The sacred fruit of the grove of Idunna was said to be the means by which the Gods retained their youth, vigour and other abilities. I had not thought that they were something that could be given out to the average mortal.

'The peaches-of-youth are not given out to the average human,' Crow replied with a raised, Mr. Spock-like eyebrow. 'They may occasionally be given to an extraordinary person who may be of special interest or use to the Old Ones.'

I sat for a moment pondering that. How incredibly amazing that such a thing might be possible! I imagined what such a thing would be capable of doing to the human physiology – perhaps healing and curing all kinds of ailments. Perhaps even reversing the aging process.

'The sacred apples are not what most people think,' Crow added. 'A person has to ponder these things deeply because as you know in the Odin Brotherhood riddles and obscure meaning are everywhere.'

After that there was much to digest, more than just the food and drink in front of me. Both of us sensed the need for a break and again focused on our refreshments.

'So as you can see the customs and traditions of the Odin Brotherhood are visible even before a person may decide to initiate,' Crow said at last, seeing that I was ready to converse again. 'One has to know where to look, of course. It is a filter.'

In my experience with them thus far, the Odin Brotherhood had indeed proven themselves more than enigmatic. I had deduced very early on that there was not only a massive amount of lore just beneath the surface, but that there were a number of filters in place to keep what they termed 'common human beings' out.

'The iceberg analogy again,' Crow replied after I had mentioned this to him. 'Yes, it's my theory as well. My contact won't talk in detail about this though. He avoids the questions. But I do know there are idiot-filters in place. Subversive-filters as well.'

I nodded my head to that. I had no doubt once again that the Brotherhood had not survived so long in a world often focused against them by being foolish.

'There are layered messages everywhere, in all of this,' Crow said. 'Like I said, you have to know where to look. In order to be prepared for initiation a person has to be aware of much more than they can find in a book or on the internet. The Odin Brotherhood are not called 'those-who-know' for no reason.'

'I see,' I said.

'After a person has passed through all of the filters - and I am not talking about the wannabes here, but the authentic people - after they have passed through the filters and after they have been suitably called, they prepare for the initiation.'

I had read all about the initiation in Dr. Mirabello's book. Those who wished to join the Odin Brotherhood, and those who were worthy, undertook a self-initiatory rite that involved isolation, a semi-fast and a symbolic blood-marking. It was not for the faint of heart or the foolish. A sacred oath was sworn at the ritual as well. It was said that the ritual combined with the oath made one a friend of the Gods – a Blood-Brother even.

'It was not always like that though,' Crow said rather mysteriously. 'Long ago, in the ancient times, people had to seek the sacred dream. It was not as it is now when the dream comes to us. People used to do things like fasting, mutilation, deprivation and even sleeping on the skins of sacred animals. Sometimes they would sit out for long periods without food or water, or hole up in a place that was considered especially sacred. They went after the dream.'

'Why did it change then?' I asked. The tradition of sitting out in the quest for a vision was familiar to me: I had known a number of Native American people who had done this, as it was an Indian tradition to seek divine knowledge in such a way.

'After the return of the Sacred Lady, the Shrouded-One-of-Odin, the tradition was changed. The dream now comes first. I am not sure why this was done exactly but I know for a fact that it was done.'

'Still, it sounds like a person needs to be powerfully inspired to finally decide that they are going to go on the Sojourn,' I said. It did not sound like a quest that a reasonable person would undertake lightly. The steps involved could be dangerous to a person not wise or experienced in the ways of the wild places. Also there was the matter of the commitment required to perform such a deed. In my opinion it was considerably beyond the grasp of most modern-day people to fully comprehend, let alone complete in a noble fashion. To this end I was convinced that relatively few had walked that Sojourn-road. I was equally convinced and suspicious that many had lied about completing the ritual, which was called the Sojourn-of-the-Brave.

'The world is full of little people who make up stories to appear better than they are,' Crow said. 'The internet especially just oozes with the bullshit made up by tough guys and wannabes. It is relatively easy to tell with most of them though and I'm sure the Odin Brotherhood has a precise way to tell.'

I too had been informed that the Odin Brotherhood had precise ways of knowing who had legitimately completed the Sojourn and those who had not. No details had been provided but when one assumes that the Odin Brotherhood has direct friendly relations with the Gods many possibilities open up.

I asked Crow what he knew of the initiation. He told me that while the most basic description appeared in Dr. Mirabello's book the reality was, once again, far deeper.

'The initiation is a deep thing,' he said. 'Like anything else with the Brotherhood it has layers of meaning; three at the least. It is dangerous as well. When a person has properly prepared and has gone out into the mountains – even then things can happen – but with the Sojourn you are opening yourself up to incredibly powerful forces. It's like grabbing onto a million volt power-line with your bare hands.'

I nodded and waited patiently for him to continue.

'So many people I have talked to ask me if it needs to be this or that exact way, and when people ask me things like that I know for a fact they aren't ready. It's not like that. You have to go with your guts as much as your heart and head into this thing. You also gotta think big picture and way outside the box.'

I thought about what he had said about layers. The Odin Brotherhood often teaches in threes. I recalled this from many hours of poring over the reams of notes and other information I had on them. To the ancient ancestors three was sacred and to many pagan people it still was. Three threes – nine - is even more sacred because it represents the cyclic nature of the universe among other things.

'These kids mostly ask me things like, "Can I make the knife out of this material or that material?" or "Can the shroud be made of cotton or hemp fibre?" or "I can't get to the woods or a mountain so is the local park good enough?"' Crow grumbled momentarily. 'Like I said, when they ask stuff like this; sure questions are good, but you get a sense that someone is not ready because they don't get it.'

'Could you explain to me what your take is on the initiation?' I asked.

Crow sat back for a moment, formulating his thoughts. Then he leaned forward again and took a sip of his brew.

'If there is one word I have to use to describe my take on the initiation I would have to say that word is instinct. Yes, there are guidelines to the Sojourn but there are only a few things that are hammered in brass, so to speak.'

'Care to fill me in?'

'There are only a few of what I would call absolutes in the Sojourn,' he said. 'As with everything the Odin Brotherhood wants people who are capable of thinking outside the box and thinking boldly. A potential member of the Brotherhood needs to be able to improvise, adapt and most of all, think multi-dimensionally. Trusting your deep instincts is a start on this road.'

I myself had read many discussions between people on internet forums in which there was much confusion as to the minute details of the Sojourn. Many were concerned with what was expected and exactly how the minutiae of the ritual were to be carried out. I once asked my Brotherhood contact about this and the response was that the Odin Brotherhood had little interest in holding anyone's hand.

It also reminded me of a time long ago in which I had asked my mentor, Ari, for details on how to perform a particular type of meditation. He had simply pointed to a mirror on the wall and said, 'I have given you the basics, now for the rest, ask the guy you see in there.' I knew that the Odin Brotherhood was uninterested in the unworthy and that indeed through the multitude of sometimes aimless questions the unworthy were constantly excluding themselves.

'I had a teacher once who told me that there is no such thing as a dumb question,' Crow said in a matter-of-fact kind of tone. 'He told me that while there was no such thing as a dumb question there was such a thing as too many questions. The reason for that is because when a person continues asking questions they are not applying themselves to the problem and want it done for them.'

'I hear you.'

'The Sojourn is sacred to Heimdall. Heimdall is a Warrior and a warder. He is gifted with the abilities of the seer,' said Crow. 'He is the son of nine mothers and this is important as well. It would be difficult to put one over on Heimdall, I think. That is one of the reasons he is connected with the ritual.'

Indeed I would not want to run afoul of Heimdall, though I suspect that he simply ignored any who attempted the Sojourn who were not worthy.

'Things will come out of the night,' Crow said. 'I have been told that. If you are successful and you have done what is appropriate you will see things. Many people are not ready for this and they have no business being out there if they are going to be deluded about what they are doing.'

'The most important aspect of the Sojourn,' he continued, 'the thing you need to get right, is the timing. The Solstices are times when the veil between worlds is thin and the dimensional spaces where the Gods dwell are most easily reached. So for this reason the Sojourn is held on one of the two Solstices. When I go I will go on the Winter Solstice because that is the time of year when Fjolnir is most often at work in Midgard.'

Fjolnir is one of the many names given to Odin, chief of the Gods of Asgard. Indeed I had heard on many occasions that winter was his preferred time to visit our world. I had not heard why that was, if anyone knew.

'Solitude and a natural place away from other humans are important,' Crow said. 'I have heard tales of Sojourns performed by others who have taken a slightly different path than this. But I think that it is the intent of neophyte and the ability to improvise and adapt that is the most important thing.'

Crow waved and got the attention of the server. When she came over he ordered himself a coffee. I thought that might be a good idea so I ordered one too.

'The other important thing is the blood-aspect of the ritual,' Crow continued. 'The shedding of blood binds the person to the oath. It also sends up a kind of cosmic signal and draws attention to the person performing the ritual.'

I nodded. It was a ritual of a very ancient design. I had no doubt that people of many cultures had understood the value of blood-letting in ritual.

'Here is something you might not know,' Crow added. 'It's the belief of the Odin Brotherhood that when a person properly conducts the Sojourn of the Brave, and completes the creation of the blood-mark, the Marks-of-Joy, then even if they might die the straw-death at a later time they will be favoured to go to the White Kingdom.'

'I did not know that,' I answered.

The White Kingdom was the term used by the Odin Brotherhood to describe the realm of the Gods of Asgard, particularly the Halls of Odin at Valhalla. In the Odinist thought of the Brotherhood there were three realms where the spirit of the deceased might travel: The White Kingdom, the Grey Kingdom and the Black Kingdom. The destination point of said spirits depended upon the manner of death, with those who had died 'ordinary' straw-deaths going to the Grey Kingdom and those who had died of unnatural means (especially sorcery) ending up in the Black Kingdom.

I found it fascinating that the taking of the Marks-of-Joy, inspired as I was told by the Marking-of-the-Spear ritual, would allow a person access to the High Halls before their death.

'Kind of like advance tickets to the afterlife,' Crow added. He was not joking; his face was quite serious. 'The members of the Odin Brotherhood believe this and it is yet another reason why they are so dead-serious about the commitment a person makes when they Sojourn.'

I thought for a moment more. I was tempted to ask for additional details but I knew that if he had them, Crow would either have revealed them to me or not, depending on his motives.

'So the Solstice timing, the solitude and the blood are the big three for you?' I asked, continuing with the earlier discussion thread.

'Yes,' he replied. 'Naturally a person should try to walk in the traditional way as much as they can. They should look to the description in the Odin Brotherhood book for inspiration and do the ritual the way it has been done for a long time.'

'So the ritual shroud, the knife, the fast and the rest of the things that are described in the Mirabello text should be looked at as an inspiration rather than hard and fast rules that need to be adhered to precisely?'

'Exactly,' he said. 'This is my take on it, of course, but they need to use their individuality and their heads when they go off on this thing. Sheep follow along blindly and the Brotherhood is not looking for that; they are looking for leaders. Fire, blood and steel are the elements that surround this ritual. It's certainly not a ritual that should be entered into by a herd animal.'

'The way of the Sojourn is the way of the traveler,' Crow added after a moment. 'It is a tracing of the way of Odin on his quest to break barriers and explore new horizons. It is, in its way, a mini-death; a person goes in one way and a part of them, the part that was holding them back, dies. It's replaced with a shining new person of sorts.'

I suggested to him that there would always be people who would go off on the Sojourn unprepared, perhaps with an attitude of arrogance or laissez faire.

His response was abrupt. 'Then, like I said, there is always the possibility that such people will meet up with some unfortunate things,' he said. 'The Odin Brotherhood does not encourage anyone to undertake the Sojourn of the Brave. They leave it up to the individual to decide whether their destiny might include this. People who go into it with an ignorant or disrespectful attitude may get way more than they bargained for.'

I too had heard stories from some people, tales in which

individuals had gone off ostensibly to perform the ritual but had been unsuccessful. These had either lied and made up fanciful stories of their experience, or had decided, probably quite wisely, to try again when they were better prepared.

'The people who succeed are the ones who have become aware of the ways of Those-Who-Know,' Crow said. 'They know nine things that they need to complete the ritual which in itself is part of a much larger circle.'

He explained these to me as he understood them:

To know the basic nature of the world and in order to
  do this the Odinist needs to re-learn how to think.

To understand that time is circular. Linear time is a lie.

That which has happened before will happen again.

To understand the nature of blood, fire, steel, silence, and the power of whispered words. To this end the Odinist understands the use of knowledge and the power of will and instinct.

To know that a true Odinist is an element of nature, an instrument of balance and a friend to the Gods.

The true Odinist embraces mystery and the nature of the continual quest.

To know that true Odinists are exceptionally rare: they understand their place in the world of the Gods and the world of men. No other human being can ever be the superior – in any way – of a member of the Odin Brotherhood.

To know that a true Odinist never kneels. He stands before his Elder Kin. He is a neo-barbarian; alive, strong and free. Cowards and weaklings kneel. Cowards and weaklings seek to rule also. A true Odinist, instead, masters himself.

To know that a true Odinist never worships or prays: he speaks to his Gods in the manner one would address a respected tribal Elder.

To know that a true Odinist sees 'faith' as a poison: a member of the Odin Brotherhood seeks truth and has *confidence in those things that are proven to him or her. In keeping with this the true Odinist follows his heart and knows the ways of the Gods and nature instinctively. He does not require man-made commandments to keep him strong and honorable.*

I asked Crow what his thoughts were on the other customs and traditions of the Odin Brotherhood. He responded that the Odin Brotherhood liked to keep things simple as their purpose was not to form a temple or a church organization. The purpose of the Brotherhood was to preserve and protect the lore as well as disseminate the Old Knowledge as widely as possible.

'As you know, other than the Sojourn, there are seasonal rites,' Crow said.

We paused for a moment as the server returned with our coffee.

'Rituals are always performed alone and at night, as you are aware,' Crow added after she left. 'All other actions are performed with what I like to think of as the three specifications. You can find them in Mirabello's book: strangers are excluded, all words to the Gods are spoken in whispers and violations of frith are forbidden.'

I had been aware of those things. I had little doubt that they had evolved as the result of the extreme need for secrecy in the early days. Strangers could constitute a security breach, loud and open vocalizations that might be overheard could attract undue attention and violations of frith could also draw attention to things better kept quiet.

'Silence and mystery are of huge importance to the Odin Brotherhood,' Crow said. 'In secrets there is power and one of the best ways to retain and shape that power is through the application of silence and mystery. One can achieve a lot if he limits access to the information he has. Doing things like this are an application of will and strength.'

I nodded and finished my glass of Guinness. I had little interest in becoming inebriated.

'The Rite-of-Bragi is performed in all of these and it is a means of communicating with the Gods. One thing that is important is that there are three sacred festivals and they are held in connection with Bragi. Bragi is the husband of Idunna, as you know, so a person has to think deeply on this fact.'

The three sacred festivals of the Odin Brotherhood are the Night-of-joy (Summer Solstice), the Night-of-Courage (at Samhain/October 31st), and the Night-of-Generosity which occurs on the eve of the Winter Solstice. The details of these festivals and their concomitant rites can of course be found in the Odin Brotherhood book authored by Mark Mirabello.

'Of course there are the death rites, the marriage and naming rites,' Crow said. 'But these we know about from Dr. Mirabello's book and other sources. I have no doubt that there are other rites that are reserved for the people who have crossed the line and done the ritual of the Sojourn.'

'Independent thought and action are encouraged,' Crow said, finishing off his coffee and putting the cup back down on the table with a flourish. 'It's why there are no designated leaders and there is no priesthood: each member is a leader and each member is also a priest.'

'I imagine that there probably are other rites and traditions,' I agreed. 'And once a member there may be certain things that are considered secret: the outside world would not be told of them.'

'The Odin Brotherhood makes no secret of the fact that they are an exclusive society,' Crow said. 'It would come as no surprise to me if there were rituals that are insider-only things. I also think there are expectations that members will do their own thing as well. People who demand that secret societies suddenly open their arms and reveal everything are in for an unpleasant surprise. Secrets hold power: mystery is the rocket fuel for the human imagination. Without these things we are no better than domestic animals.'

'Calculated clues of misdirection,' I chimed in. Those had been the exact words of my contact in the Odin Brotherhood when he had been describing the mystery aspect of the tradition.

I agreed once again with my enigmatic friend. I had little doubt that should he go on the Sojourn he would make a valuable addition to the ranks of the Odin Brotherhood. I was certain that the Odin Brotherhood by now knew it as well. He already knew far more than I did about their traditions and from what I could gather he had not been on his quest much longer than I had.

'So we have covered the idea of rituals,' Crow said. 'The Odin Brotherhood is not big on having a whole lot of them as we already discussed. They are about deeds more than words, which is as it should be.'

'Preserving the lore,' I added.

'Yes,' he replied. 'It's all about the lore.'

I recalled reading an interesting piece once, by a person who called himself a friend of the Odin Brotherhood. He had said that if he could distil everything he knew about the Odin Brotherhood down into one idea it would be 'the Lore.' I had to agree with that. It was the primary focus and indeed the reason for the Brotherhood's existence in the first place.

'Let's talk about some of the other customs of the Brotherhood,' Crow said. 'Maybe we can walk some of this meal off on the trails.'

The university campus is surrounded by a substantial coastal forest known as the University Endowment Lands. There has been little development in the large stands of cedar, pine and Douglas fir, save for a network of nature trails that stretch many kilometres.

Often the trails are populated by people walking or jogging or otherwise enjoying the deep green. However, as Crow and I made our way to the perimeter of one of the main trails we did so in the dark of evening. The forest was, for the most part, silent and the music of treetops waving high in the breeze greeted us as we entered a darkened path.

'This leads to the main cut,' Crow said.

I was familiar with it; a large road-like passage that had been cut east to west through a southern section of the forest. At one time, long ago, it had been created to accommodate power lines heading to the university but now it was a wide, groomed path that made its way between the now midnight-black walls of forest trees.

Our trail through the deepest dark was brief and we emerged on the large cut without incident. As I looked ahead, toward the west, I saw that a brilliant three quarter moon had come out and was illuminating the wide trail in glowing silver light. It was a good evening: stars twinkled above and a slight breeze whispered through the lower levels bringing the scents of cedar and earth.

Crow stepped onto the trail and we walked toward the west where ultimately the university lay.

'The Odin Brotherhood uses runes for divination,' Crow said. 'Only the Younger Futhark is used because it was the runic system in use at the time of the widow.'

'I have heard this,' I replied. 'The Younger Futhark consists of sixteen runes as opposed to the twenty four runes used in the Elder Futhark.'

'Yes,' Crow said. 'There is a lot to this, according to my contact. The runes are not simply symbols to be interpreted at random; they are not some New-Age thing like so many think they are. They are powerful guides to the nature of the multiverse.'

I nodded and waited for him to continue.

'There are prophecies and deep mysteries that the Odin Brotherhood holds and the keys to many of these can be found in the enigma of the runes. Look to the constellations in the sky and you will see the runes there. They will outlast any stone on earth and they are very significant.'

'I have heard of some of these prophecies,' I said.

Crow put up a finger and smiled. 'Yeah, and if we start talking about those we will be side tracked all night.'

I smiled back in the silver moonlight. I certainly knew how our conversations had a tendency to go off on tangents.

'Runes are for the most part misunderstood by modern people,' he said. 'Have you ever heard the saying, "just enough knowledge to be dangerous"?'

I nodded. I had heard it many times in my life.

'Well, that's what a lot of people have going on when they play with runes in a disrespectful way,' he said. 'To the Odin Brotherhood runes are deeply sacred and connected to Odin and Mimir. They are powerful keys and also teachers. They play an important role in the Odin Brotherhood though I haven't been able to get a lot of information on the details of their use within the Brotherhood.'

We walked in silence for a moment. I was glad of such small pauses in the conversation because they were good for personal processing of information.

'The runes must be cut from the wood of fruit-bearing trees,' Crow continued. 'They should be cut with a sharp blade, marked with blood and dedicated at night. They should be kept in a dark place when they are not in use and, as a matter of fact, I have heard that members of the Brotherhood prefer to read the runes only at night.'

'I will talk more about prophecies later but I believe the runes play an important part in the unravelling of these mysteries,' he added. 'There are instructions as well in the Hávamál and other sources.'

'Do you have a set of runes?' I asked.

'Do you?' he counter-questioned.

I told him that I did, though they were the runes of the Elder, not the Younger, Futhark.

'I have a set,' he replied finally. 'They are cherry wood.'

'The runes are more than personal oracles,' Crow said as we stepped over a small stream that had flooded across the trail. 'They are seen by the Odin Brotherhood as conduits to mystery, almost like a kind of 1-800 line that a person can use to connect to the Norns. It is for that reason they should be used with deep respect.'

My own set of runes was carved from stone, and as I have said, was in the form of the Elder Futhark. I had carved them and dedicated them myself over a nine day period. I understood their power: they had shown it to me. I suspected that the Odin Brotherhood would see the runes as sacred things as well.

'One of the uses the Odin Brotherhood has for the runes is rather necromantic in nature,' Crow said. 'But that is no surprise when you consider the story of the origin of the Brotherhood. It is said that if they are properly used at night, the runes can be utilized to get yes or no answers from the recently dead.'

'Similar to the widow,' I said.

'Maybe not as advanced as the ritual of the Shrouded-One,' he replied. 'But yes, something like that.'

'Interesting,' I said.

It was all I could think of to say at the moment. I realized that there was a lot I did not know. I also realized that if Crow, who denied membership in the Odin Brotherhood, admittedly knew little (and he knew a lot more than I did), then there was probably a very large body of unknown lore floating around, waiting for the right people to find it.

'Okay, you wanted to hear about the icons and idols,' Crow began.

My attention, already focused, became more so and I told him that indeed I did.

'First let me tell you that since the Odin Brotherhood is all about the lore, members of the Brotherhood are expected to preserve and spread the lore. There are many ways to do this but one thing that every member is supposed to do before they die is to create a stash of books and lore. They are supposed to make this stash as indestructible as they can by carefully selecting what materials are used and how it is contained. Then they are supposed to bury or hide it so that one day it might be found and used by someone in a future generation.'

'Like a time capsule,' I suggested.

'A lot like that, yeah,' he answered. 'So knowing that we also know that every member of the Odin Brotherhood is supposed to teach at least one other person the ways of the tradition before he dies.'

I had not known that but it made perfect sense. In addition to spreading and preserving the lore, each new member would add more and more chances that the lore would be preserved.

'So when you consider these things you also have to consider that the lore is not always conveyed in the form of books or printed papers,' Crow continued. 'Some of these ways of conveyance are easily recognizable; they are tapes or discs....maybe even pictures or things like that. Other things, however, carry with them deep secrets and the potential to do terrible things if they were to end up in the wrong hands.'

'So then these things are not supposed to be used by people outside the Brotherhood?' I asked, more and more intrigued by the moment.

'That's right,' he said. 'Some things are kind of like life-boats; packages buried or hidden with the hope that one day they might be discovered and used by the right kind of person. Other things are of a different nature and are designed to communicate information of a different sort.'

'That's where the icons come in,' I speculated.

'Yes,' he said. 'There are people who think that the Odin Brotherhood is just about ideas and legends but they are showing themselves to know little if they do. There are artifacts in the Brotherhood that have been in circulation a very long time. They are often warded by particular members and sometimes they are passed down from teacher to student in a traditional way. The most powerful of these things are called icons.'

'Sounds impressive,' I said. Again I was not so far along to think that the Odin Brotherhood might have such things, but it made a lot of sense.

'There is a lot more to the Odin Brotherhood than you might think,' Crow said. 'I have heard stories of members who are of high position in society. I have also heard that there are members from every walk of life, all working to preserve the lore and in their way help to re-balance our world.'

'There are ancient books – tomes, out there as well,' Crow said. 'What they contain I have no idea but you know I have had a few ideas, like maybe they are lost Sagas or Eddas; maybe something really pivotal to the world as we know it.'

I immediately thought of the Codex Regius, that work of lore most prized by the Odin Brotherhood. I recall reading that there were eight pages, possibly more, that had been removed from the original document. No one knew of their whereabouts. I had immediately assumed that perhaps they had been destroyed by agents of the church in the old days. However, I started thinking that maybe they had found their way...elsewhere?

'I was told that Snorri Sturlsson was a secret pagan,' Crow continued. 'That is the belief of the Odin Brotherhood. Remember that they believe the best way to hide something is in plain sight so it would make sense that Snorri, labouring under the guise of a simple historian, was preserving the lore right under the noses of the Christian authorities of his time. I was thinking that perhaps some of his works might also have been preserved in a secret way.'

It was most definitely food for thought. 'And the talismans you spoke of?' I inquired.

'That is a very grey area,' Crow replied. 'All I was told was that there are items of power at large in the world and many of them are of potent Odinic import. I was told that many people who walk around claiming to be Odinists would be frightened or even harmed if they were ever to come into contact with any of these items of power. I was told it is the job of those-who-know to be ever watchful for the arrival of such things into their lives.'

'That's it?'

'That's as much as I know about talismans,' he said.

'What about these icons?' I asked, getting back to the original subject.

'The icons are idols,' he replied. 'I was told that they are artifacts of great power. They are very, very old and there are quite a number of them. They were saved from the pillaging acts of the church and others over time. Some have been acquired through various trusts and agents over the centuries as well. The idea is that the Old Ways might be preserved. The enemy was not successful in destroying nearly as much as they thought they had.'

I was fascinated. I had been wondering to what depths the fabric of the Odin Brotherhood had spread into the history of the world, but I had, again, not considered the possibility of such artifacts. However I was also very pleased to hear that they had been successful in preserving so much more than many suspected.

'My contact confided to me that these icons were very strange and otherworldly. He told me that they were carved from wood and made in the shape of pillars.'

'He confided this to you?' I asked. I was concerned that Crow might be breaking a confidence.

Crow turned and regarded me briefly as we walked. He knew exactly what I was thinking because he assured me that no trust was being breached.

'I was told that I may pass on this information to someone I found worthy,' he said.

I grinned. It was nice to be found worthy.

'These icons were for the most part not made by humans,' Crow said dryly. 'I was told that they were, in fact, made by Gods or others like them. A few made by ordinary people, but for the most part they were created by Elder Ones and given to favoured heroes. Some are said to have fallen from Asgard as well.'

'They must be magnificent to see,' I said. I could only imagine the level of craftsmanship that one might observe in the works of an advanced being.

'Yeah, about that...' Crow began with an odd cynical look on his face. 'Apparently these icons are not made to be seen at all – at least by us humans. I was told that the icons contain such great power that if an ordinary person, not properly prepared, was to look at one they would be driven mad or even killed by the experience.'

'A properly prepared person?' I asked.

'That's what I was told,' he said. 'A properly prepared person. I think that this would be a person favoured by the Elder Ones to look at and use the object. Maybe a very wise member of the Brotherhood. I am not certain.'

Something powerful enough to drive a person crazy or kill them was no laughing matter. I imagined that things like this would be carefully guarded by the Odin Brotherhood, perhaps kept in a vault or a hidden secured location somewhere.

'Interestingly enough, sometimes the icons are shipped around to various members. Others are kept in certain locations. They are supposedly kept in strong-boxes,' Crow said. 'I was informed that viewing the icons themselves was a very special privilege that was reserved for specific people at particular times – and this under particular conditions.'

'I imagine so,' I said. 'I guess that there would be certain respected wise-people among the Brotherhood who would be able to determine who these particular people were and at which times and which circumstances the icons might be viewed.'

'That's the impression I get,' Crow said. 'I wasn't told a lot beyond that, but I will tell you that sometimes members are given icons for safe-keeping. I have absolutely no idea why this would be but I was very sternly warned that if I was ever to receive such a strong-box I was never to open it until I was prepared by the Gods.'

I found that curious.

'Prepared by the Gods, how?' I asked.

'Your guess is as good as mine, buddy,' he replied. 'I was told that in some cases a representative of the Brotherhood might at the appropriate time come and take the box along on its way, or that I might become a keeper of the box and that I should make sure the box was passed on to a trustworthy person at the end of my own life here in Midgard.'

'You were certainly right,' I said. 'The Odin Brotherhood sure contains its share of mysteries.'

'Not to say that I would ever receive such a box,' Crow added. 'I am not even a member of the Odin Brotherhood.'

'That goes without saying,' I replied.

We walked along the trail for a distance until eventually we ended up on another path leading toward the university. I realized that we had covered a considerable distance and it would not be long until we began encountering the street lights of the campus perimeter.

Crow suddenly stopped and looked at his watch. He had to squint for a moment in the dim light, and then:

'Did you know it's quarter after ten?' he asked, rather incredulously.

I too had lost track of the time. I told him that I had no idea it was that late.

'I have the feeling that there are a lot of other things we will be talking about before we're done,' he smiled. 'But I need to get going soon.'

I agreed. It was getting late.

Crow changed the subject completely and started talking about hockey. I was impressed with how seamlessly he could shift mental gears, even from such heady stuff as we had covered to the relatively mundane – with the greatest of ease.

I had much to think about, obviously, but I set it aside in my head as best I could and accommodated the new essence of the conversation.

About twenty minutes later, we emerged from a trail onto a quiet street not far from some student residence buildings. It would be a relatively short walk from there to where I could catch a cab or a bus home.

We walked together until we reached a much busier road. There we waited for the crossing light to change. I looked up and noticed a group of grey clouds moving ominously in from the Pacific Ocean, to the west.

'Looks like rain,' I said.

I suddenly turned and looked around me. Crow was gone. He had silently walked away without so much as a 'see you later.'

The first droplets began to fall, first as a near-mist but after a moment, as full-on rain. I picked up the pace in the hopes that I could make it home before I became really wet.

No doubt I would hear from the mysterious Crow again sometime soon...when he was ready.

6

Prophecies

'You are very predictable in some ways,' Crow said as he suddenly appeared, seemingly out of nowhere, and sat down at the table.

I was seated in a study area in one of the university's many libraries. It was late. 'I do have a tendency to use one or two libraries out here more than the rest,' I replied.

'It has been the better part of a year since we first met,' he said, setting his ever familiar pack on the floor and settling into a seat.

The hooded pullover was different though; it was an attractive south-western Native pattern in greens and browns. Other than that he was just as I remembered him.

As was his usual pattern, Crow had disappeared off the map for approximately two months. Where he went during that time or what his personal life was I had no idea. Out of respect I had never asked. He was correct in his estimates though; it was August, the better part of a year since we had first met.

'I remember you appearing out of nowhere then too,' I said.

He smiled. It was a cross between a genuine smile and a crafty grin – like a kid who has just recently raided a cookie jar.

'How is the book coming?' he asked.

'Well,' I replied. 'I will have to let you read it when it's done.'

'That would be cool,' he said. 'I don't have a lot of time tonight but I figured that since I haven't seen you in awhile I would track you down for a bit.'

I set aside the book I was reading and pushed my notebook to one side. Crow had that look about him: that look that said 'I am ready to talk if you are ready to listen.' I felt like a journalist at times around him even though I am not.

Luckily for me I had made it a habit to carry my audio recorder around with me in my pack. It had come in very handy in the past in helping my memory where our conversations were concerned.

I pulled the device out and motioned to it. He nodded and smiled as I put the thing down on the table between us.

'Did you erase those other tapes?' he asked, curiously.

'Not yet,' I replied. 'But I will once the book is finished.'

'Scout's honor, right?'

'You got it,' I said. Our agreement had been that I would be allowed to make audio recordings for the sake of accuracy, but I was to erase or destroy the recordings afterward. Crow had also said that he wished no photographs or video during our times together. I had accepted his requests and fully planned, as I had told him, to erase the tapes after we were done.

I looked at him for a second. 'You never were a Boy Scout, were you?'

'Nope, but you were,' he replied.

I found that intriguing because indeed I had been a Boy Scout once, long ago. I wondered if his knowledge of me came from some clandestine source or was simply a good guess. I decided not to bother asking for clarification because it was unlikely he would provide it anyway...other than in some enigmatic way. Besides, he had told me his time was limited and I did not want to waste it in idle banter.

Crow started right in.

'You know that the contacts between the Gods and people here in Midgard are becoming more frequent,' he said. 'As a matter of fact I think the incidences of it happening that I know of have more than doubled in the last ten years.'

I was not overly surprised. Human kind had been doing a rather efficient job of wrecking the environment over the past century in particular. The lore which spoke of the Elder Ones returning to correct the balance seemed to be proving true.

'The Odin Brotherhood long ago declared itself the enemy of slavery,' he said. 'This is also the opinion of the folk of Asgard, who revile the ones who try to steal freedom.'

'I agree with that,' I replied.

'To take freedom is to steal life. The Gods will not stand by and watch poisonous creatures gradually steal freedom all over the world,' Crow said. 'For some time there was a hope of freedom, more freedom than the world had ever seen. Much of this hope was with the so-called First-World countries, but I see now that even the United States is decaying towards some kind of police state.'

I saw where he was coming from. The world was indeed not the realm of democracy and freedom I had hoped it would develop into. Various religious movements combined with the insidious touch of modern day corporate culture had seen to that.

'The Odin Brotherhood is not overly concerned with politics or with nationalist movements because they have survived worse and they think in terms of centuries,' Crow said. 'But now the behavior of humankind has really been causing damage to Midgard. It must be stopped.'

'I agree one hundred percent,' I replied.

Crow reached into his bag and extracted an old, battered green thermos. He opened the lid and the smell of coffee filled the air. He poured a cupful into the lid and then pulled another small cup from his bag.

'Coffee?' he asked.

I declined politely. I had been in the library for a considerable time already and had consumed numerous cups of coffee during the day. I had had enough.

'There are prophecies in the Odin Brotherhood,' he said, after taking a sip from his cup. 'The world is about to change and this has been spoken of long ago.'

The concept of the 'change-of-times' was not unknown to me. It was a thing that more and more people were coming to realize: sages and Elders from many cultures were coming forth with warnings. Indeed I had known personally of a great number of prophecies coming from Native American and African cultures concerning this.

'Do you think it will be Ragnarök?' I asked pensively. It was the Norse word for the colossal battle between the Gods and their enemies: an end to the world as we know it and the beginning of a new one in the aftermath.

'No,' he replied. 'But I do think that this is a time of really big changes and these changes are pretty much on our doorstep as we speak. All the more reason for the Odin Brotherhood to seek the worthy for its ranks.'

'So in the minds of the Odin Brotherhood members the time of Ragnarök is not yet here?' I asked.

'It's my opinion that Ragnarök is not yet here,' Crow replied. 'But I get the impression that there are those in the Brotherhood that agree with me. This will be a time where humans are able to pull back from the edge that we have been pushed to through the greed and darkness of a small percentage of people. It will be a time for the "real" people of the Earth to eliminate those who have been abusing them and the world. It will be a time to heal.'

I found it fascinating to see that there was so much synchronicity between what Crow had just said and what I had heard from a number of other sources. The Elders of many cultures had said just as much: that this would be a time for correction and healing, and that the few who had for so long manipulated the world would no longer be permitted to do so.

'The Odin Brotherhood believes that we are entering what they have called the Wolf-Age,' Crow said grimly. 'It will be an age of hardship and reckoning. Millions, perhaps billions even, will die because the earth can no longer support the size of the population.'

'And you think this will be a good thing?' I asked.

Crow leaned a ways across the table and fixed me with his gaze for a long moment. There was a predatory animal in there behind those eyes. It was a very old-world essence and at times like this I could sense it quite clearly near the surface.

'I think it will be an excellent thing,' he said finally. 'The root problems of the world are found in overpopulation and the needs of a few twisted groups who think they have a right to rule the many.'

'I see,' I said.

'It is very important that those who feel the need to act, do so in these times. By act I mean that they should do what they need in order to see to the safety and comfort of their families and immediate kin,' Crow said. 'Those of the Odin Brotherhood have said that what has happened before will happen again. They prepare for such a thing now.'

What he was saying sounded ominous. I told him so.

'It's reality, my friend,' he replied. 'It's also one of the reasons why I met you and why I am passing on to you what I know. It's also because I think that the world needs another book about the Odin Brotherhood – one that is, in a sense, approved by them and one that will maybe get more people interested in the path of those-who-know.'

'The Odin Brotherhood favours autonomy on many levels,' I said. 'I would not go so far as to say that they approve of my project so much as they encourage individual initiative. If my book serves them then I guess they will be pleased.'

'It helps to preserve the lore,' he replied. 'They know you are writing it and I have no doubt they think this is a good thing.'

We sat for a moment in silence, absorbed in thought and surrounded by the soft sounds found in the quiet of libraries.

'Corruption is natural,' Crow began. 'Time and corruption go hand in hand and the Odin Brotherhood looks at it exactly the same way as I do. Believe me, I have had considerable talks with my contact about this.'

Crow leaned back and took a big sip of his coffee. 'The way the modern world is going is not good,' he said. 'The Odin Brotherhood considers this age we are currently on the verge of leaving to be decadent and weak.'

I was reminded of something my own contact had told me not long ago regarding modern society. He said, *Societies which become overly open and distribute unearned rights and privilege are sowing the seeds of their demise.*

I told this to Crow and he heartily agreed.

'There are way too many people and it seems that the more there are the more twisted things become. The Odin Brotherhood sees where all of this is leading. Did you know that they even hope that one day members may join in on missions to colonize other worlds? That way the lore would be spread and preserved away from the earth.'

That was a bit of information that I had not known. As with many things I heard regarding the Odin Brotherhood, it made sense: spread the lore.

'If we survive long enough to get so far as colonization,' I answered.

'The Odin Brotherhood has people in some pretty influential places I think,' Crow said. 'I hope that they will be able to be of some help in that way. I want our species to clean up its act and survive.'

'I hope so too,' I said.

'Time is a circle,' Crow said after a moment. 'The Odin Brotherhood looks at it like this: the universe begins all fresh and green in a kind of golden age. Eventually it all ages and becomes corrupt. The result of this corruption is that we enter a Wolf-Age which is a prelude to the much greater Time-of-Winter. A purifying destruction follows the time of winter and this is eventually followed by a clean green renewal.'

Crow leaned forward again and was silent for a moment. A library assistant glided by with a rolling cart full of books.

'The next universe, just like the one we are in right now, will eventually become corrupt as well and the cycle will continue. And a wise man once said, "The pink blossom becomes the brown flower, which dies, and through it a new seed is born." This is why the Odin Brotherhood looks to what they call the 'religion of the Eddas,' the Codex Regius in particular,' Crow said. 'This is because they believe that these works come from the last, fresh healthy barbarians of Europe. As such they see it as the least corrupted.'

'Is it just the lore of the Eddas then?' I asked. I had heard otherwise but I wanted to hear Crow's take on it.

'The Odin Brotherhood studies many bodies of lore,' he replied.

'Lore and culture from all over the world because in knowledge there is wisdom. However, they study the Eddaic verses in the most depth because they believe them to be the purest. They believe that they are most deeply connected to the Indo-Europeans because the Indo-Europeans were and are a people of the Earth. The Odin Brotherhood believes that all people of the Earth in their various races and cultures have the ability to be great. The Odin Brotherhood, because it was founded in Europe, focuses its culture and tradition around that.'

I understood what he was saying. I agreed with that as well. All people everywhere had the potential to be great and those the world over, who were re-awakening to their deep-Earth traditions and their Elder Gods, were realizing that.

'Nobody is born special or great,' Crow said. 'The Odin Brotherhood doesn't see any particular race of humans as being superior to the other either. The Odin Brotherhood recognizes that each person can decide to strive for greatness or not. Each person can decide to wake up or not. The Odin Brotherhood is about struggle and awakening. There is no thought to lineage or the like either. If you have great ancestors but you yourself are a lazy weakling, you are not noble.'

I sat for a moment longer, pondering what he had said. It seemed to me that there was more he wanted to say but for some reason was having some difficulty in articulating it. He seemed almost frustrated with this fact and though he tried to conceal it beneath his usual façade I could sense it.

'So,' I began, changing tracks a little, 'Times are changing and the Odin Brotherhood calls to those of great potential to join them. They plan to weather the coming storms while preserving the lore.'

'Yes,' he said, eyeing me with a raised eyebrow. He was curious as to the way I had phrased my last.

'I was curious as to what your take on the future of the Odin

Brotherhood is. I wonder if they have told you of any future plans you can speak about?'

The eyebrow returned to the same level as its companion. The semi-grin returned to Crow's face. It was enigmatic; there were times when I could not determine if that look was borne of humour, sarcasm or wry amusement.

'You know the Odinist prophecy which states "When the world is pregnant with lies, a secret long hidden will be revealed." Well, we are quickly reaching that point where the world is thick with BS,' Crow replied. 'I think we have ways to go yet before it reaches a critical point, but that day is coming.'

He reached over and took a sip of his coffee.

'The Brotherhood makes plans and has been making plans for a very long time,' he said. 'They plan to do whatever they can to keep with their purposes of protecting and disseminating the lore, but beyond that I know they will play a part in helping to heal the Earth. That's important because ultimately, as I said, they plan to have members off-world in other places so that the lore will be further spread and protected.'

'The Brotherhood sees things long term,' I said.

'Yes, they think in centuries,' he added.

'The Gods are returning more and more,' Crow said. He had said this before during our talks. 'Some think it is because they tire of seeing Midgard ruined through the efforts of a relative few; ignorant fools who seek only power. I think that this is part of the prophecy; the secret long hidden that will be revealed.'

'It is the prophecy of Nanna, the wife of Balder,' I said. I was reminded again of the strange synchronicity between the teachings and prophecies of the Odin Brotherhood and teachers I had learned from. Supposedly none of these others had been members of the Brotherhood and of them all, Max had been the only one I knew with knowledge of them, yet there were the interesting similarities in their words.

Ari had said to me on more than one occasion, *When there is sufficient darkness in the world the light of the Gods will be revealed.*' It sounded very similar to the Odinist prophecy that Crow and I had been speaking about.

Crow nodded when I pointed this out to him.

'You know the legend of the Mountain-of-Promise,' he said. 'This is covered in the original book.'

The legend of the Mountain-of-Promise is the Odin Brotherhood prophecy that tells of the burial place of the three founders of the tradition. It is a hidden mound which contains three large golden monoliths as well as a trove of hidden knowledge. The legend tells us that when the time is right and this secret place is finally discovered, great truths will be revealed.

'The discovery of the mountain and its cache of knowledge will be a part of that future for the Odin Brotherhood. It may be the thing that staves off Ragnarök for a time, at least, and in that time they will have the opportunity to continue their work.'

'Yet I have heard that while Odinists such as these are still in Midgard, Ragnarök will be postponed,' I suggested.

'Discovery of the Mountain-of-Promise will help in that,' he replied. 'I have been told that the contents of that hidden mound are world-changing.'

He did not elaborate on this, so I asked him. He told me that he did not know much more beyond that.

'Another reason that the Odin Brotherhood will not die off, as so many other similar traditions have, is because their contact with the Gods is a regular thing,' Crow said. 'I have been told that there are members who have fairly consistent contact with the Elder Ones. They do not make too much of this public though, because, well, you know how the mainstream public reacts to hearing things like that.'

'Regular contact with Gods or Goddesses?' I asked. I had

imagined it would be a special kind of event to find oneself in the company of Elder Kin.

'Yes,' he replied. 'It is not so uncommon as people think. Mundane people are too caught up in the omnipotent, unreachable God thing. It doesn't occur to them that our Gods are quite real and take an interest in our lives and our planet.'

I took a moment to absorb that.

'I have heard that some members of the Odin Brotherhood are seekers of the sacred mountain,' he said, shifting track a bit. 'Maybe one day soon one of them will find it.'

I had suspected that there might be those who would go looking for the sacred mountain. 'Would you say that perhaps there might be a kind of sub-order within the Odin Brotherhood that has it as their quest to look for the sacred mountain?' I asked.

'I have no idea about that,' he replied. 'But if we go back to that iceberg analogy you get the same idea that I have: that the Odin Brotherhood that has been revealed to the world is just a tiny tip of ice sticking out above the sea of reality. There is a lot more there than we know.'

Crow refilled his coffee cup. Again he made me the offer of some, but I grinned and politely waved it off. If he had limited time I had no interest in wasting any of it by running off to the bathroom during it.

'It is important for members of the Odin Brotherhood to be seekers at heart,' Crow said. 'Curiosity and a love of mystery are essential parts of the Odin Brotherhood. There is no place in their world for the dull-minded or those who have no sense of humor.'

Crow sat back and finished his newly poured coffee off in a single gulp. He made a refreshed 'ah' sound as he screwed the lid back on the thermos and placed it back in his bag.

'Unfortunately I have places to be and people to see,' he said. 'Aegir waits for nobody.'

I was, of course, very interested in what he meant by that but I decided not to ask.

'I'm glad I caught up with you to talk for a bit,' he said. 'It was bothering me that I hadn't covered some of that before now. I was hoping it might explain why the Odin Brotherhood is so much more visible than it used to be.'

'They see it as time is short,' I suggested.

'Yes,' he said. 'That is exactly it. They are looking to gather worthy people to preserve the lore for the dark times ahead. You are helping them do that, you know, with your book. Member or not you are doing something good.'

Crow stood up rather abruptly, looking at his watch as he did so. 'And speaking of time being short, I need to take off,' he said.

'Just going to disappear again for months on end, aren't you?' I asked, grinning. I had not forgotten his interesting disappearing act at the end of our last meeting.

He shouldered his pack. 'Nope. I am just going to walk out that door and outside. Like I said, I have someone to meet.'

With that he raised his hand in a 'goodbye' salute, and turned and left. Indeed I watched him walk all the way down the space between the stacks until he disappeared into the stairway.

I wondered who he was going to meet. I suspected that had it been of importance to me he would have told me.

I took a moment to reflect before pulling my notepad and book back in front of me.

We certainly are living in the last vestiges of a decaying age, I thought. I could fully understand why the Odin Brotherhood had decided to make its existence known. I also wondered what the real connection between Crow and the Brotherhood was, for it seemed that indeed he had appeared in my life at a most opportune time.

I suspected that such questions would never be answered. I went back to work.

7

Realms

Thunder crashed down in a deafening roar, followed by ever-increasing sheets of cold, autumn rain as I made my way quickly along the sidewalk and then down toward the building's end. Had I not been wearing an overcoat and hat I was sure I would have been soaked through in the time it took me to get from the taxi to the shelter of the staircase I was heading for.

In some places October is a time of frost in the air and perhaps the first winter snows. Vancouver however is a Lady of a different style and her version of winter is often fraught with plenty of Pacific coast rain. Thunderstorms were not so frequent though, and I counted it as just my luck to be caught out in one of them.

Checking my watch I realized I had made it to the designated place on time: a somewhat secluded little pub and restaurant nestled up against the foot of the local mountains. I walked down the stairs and entered through the large oak and brass doors. It only took a moment to pick out a familiar figure reclining in a comfortable chair near the window. 'Right out in the open this time, are you?' I asked, taking off my wet overcoat.

'I am hidden in plain sight,' Crow replied humorously.

I sat down and found a pint of something dark sitting before me – Crow's treat. I thanked him, had a sip and reclined into the comfortable chair.

'It has been a while,' he said, starting the conversation.

Indeed it had not been quite as long as his usual break between meetings. I told him I was rather surprised.

His response lacked the usual glow of wry humour that I had come to know as his trademark. 'The clock is ticking, my friend,' he said dryly. 'There is only so much time we have left and I wanted to share with you as much as I can before Solstice.'

Ah, now this made sense to me. I had suspected that Crow would eventually make the decision to walk the way of the Sojourn; to initiate into the Odin Brotherhood.

'So you consider heading into the mountains, do you?' I asked, trying to be cryptic.

'Many things happen at Solstice,' he replied. 'But I am not too interested in talking about that at this time.'

'I understand that,' I said.

Assuming that Crow was planning to undertake the Sojourn it would make sense that he did not want to provide details. After all, I am not a member of the Odin Brotherhood and the members of said tradition keep their identities secret from outsiders. It was a measure of trust that he would tell me as much as he did, even though I had not pried and did not even know what his real name was.

I settled back into my chair with a smile.

'What did you want to talk about today?' I asked.

'Realms and realities,' he replied. 'Over the last while we have covered a lot of ground but I feel like I haven't gotten the Odinist world-view completely across. I mean the Odinist world-view as the Odin Brotherhood interprets it. I have learned a lot about that point of view over the last couple of years and I wanted to share what I know.'

I had already gotten a much clearer idea of the ways of the Odin Brotherhood through Crow and a lot of that included portions of the Brotherhood's cosmology and viewpoint. I told him this and he replied that he wanted to be clear on certain things, not only from what he had learned but from how he was sure these things were related to by the Odin Brotherhood.

'The bottom line is that everything natural is in its way alive,' he began. 'It's all a part of that energy that connects everything else.

Not everything is conscious or anything like that, but the energy is there.'

His thinking was much like my own home-grown version of pagan animism. It made sense that many things would be connected in the matrix of life.

'There are what we think of as the Nine Worlds,' he continued. 'But most pagan people think of this like there are nine planets out there somewhere. I don't believe that is so. The Brotherhood's take on it is that they are alternate realities. The place we live, Midgard, is just one of them and even here there is a ton which we cannot see.'

'I was told once that the Gods inhabit oblique corridors of reality,' I said.

'That's one way of looking at it for sure,' he grinned. 'Everything is about balance. Nature is about balance and things that fall out of balance are either corrected or eliminated. That's the way it is.'

I nodded.

'Another way that a lot of modern day pagans think is that the old stories are all embellished or made-up folk tales. They think that things like the Dwarves and Elvish people are imaginary. I am here to tell you that like the Gods themselves, they are not imaginary or symbolic or figments of somebody's fantasy.'

'So what you are saying then is that the Odin Brotherhood views the multiverse, if you will, as essentially alive, cyclical and balanced. That there are multiple realities within this multiverse and that many of the things which people may dismiss as folklore are quite real,' I paraphrased.

'Yes,' he said. 'The Gods and Goddesses, the Elder Kin, are quite real and come here in physical form so why in the world wouldn't the other things be real as well?'

I suggested that in the modern world perhaps the Earth-spirits and other intelligences, termed Vaettir by the Nordic folk, were more scarce because of development and population.

'People have been so thoroughly brainwashed as kids that by

the time they grow up and can think for themselves they are hooked into the herd-think of the mainstream. It's common enough practice to steal the magic out of the lives of children at an early age these days. I guess I am not too surprised that so many can't see the things that are all around them.'

'Elves and Dwarves and the like would not be a common sight on the city streets,' I said.

'There was a time, long ago, when such a thing probably was common,' he said. 'But over time many of the fair folk and others have stepped elsewhere. That is, they have gone away from modern day humans for the most part. I think they were disgusted with what we are doing to this planet and went back to their own realms.'

'Like Svartalfheim for instance?' I asked.

'Yes,' he said. 'But there are those who stayed, many more than the average Joe-pagan would imagine. Like the Gods and Goddesses who are returning more and more, these folk are also here to communicate, if we let them. Some are more connected to their home-realm, while others are more connected to Midgard. When approached properly and with respect they can have a lot to teach.'

'And these other people; can they be approached with things like offerings and libations?' I asked. I was curious to know if the Odin Brotherhood had customs similar to many other pagan cultures.

'I have never been told of any specific ways of doing this through my contacts but it makes sense, since they walk in the Old Ways and are connected deeply to the Earth. I will tell you that I believe this and walk like this too.'

'Önd, Oðr, & Lá,' I added. 'Everything is connected.'

'Exactly,' he said.

Önd, Oðr, & Lá were the Nordic concepts of life-energy. Önd being the life-force or vital breath: the literal breath of life as passed to humankind. Oðr is the gift of consciousness and will, and Lá, which means vital fluid, describes blood, health and spiritual energy. These gifts were given to humankind, according to the lore, by Odin and his brothers Vili and Vé at the time when the first humans, Ask and Embla, were created.

'So since everything is connected it is important to work to keep things in balance,' Crow said. 'It's important that an Odinist make a good connection with nature and with the Other-folk that are out there. It's also important that an Odinist set an example of balance in themselves by living as clean and healthy a life as they can.'

'Which explains us sitting here drinking beer, eh?' I grinned sarcastically.

'Well, we are not Buddhist monks after all,' Crow grinned also. 'We need to open up and enjoy life and the now as much as we can too because we do not pine away for the afterlife like others do; we live!'

Crow paused for a brief moment. 'The real Odinist embraces the life that he is given right here and now, as I just said,' he remarked. 'The next phase will come when we die but the Gods will not be pleased with those who have wasted their lives waiting for the next one. So sure it's okay to enjoy a beer or two and to get out and have adventure in life; take a few risks, reap a few victories, if you know what I mean.'

I did. I told him so.

'Yet even in that we need to make sure we are in balance,' he said. 'How can we be of use to the Old Ones if we are of no use to ourselves in the first place?'

'So it is finding that middle ground in between?'

'Kind of, yes,' he replied. 'The idea is that each Odinist should follow his or her own heart as much as possible, and if that person has a close connection with the Gods and the Earth then balance should come of it.'

I had heard him use the terms 'true' or 'real' Odinist a few times and I decided to ask him about that.

He paused a moment before answering, but this was because he was drinking from his glass. I suspect that he had no need to formulate his response.

'When I say that, I mean a person who is cut from the fabric of the deep Earth of Midgard. I mean someone who is strong and free in his heart and who wants to live a life that is something great: somebody who wants to leave a legacy.'

I had suspected that this was the kind of thing he was getting at when he used the term. There had always been a little bit of extra passion in his words when he had used the term 'real' Odinist before. I had noted that.

'A real Odinist walks in the way of the neo-barbarian,' Crow said proudly. 'He is a creature of nature and a friend to the Gods. He is not the least bit interested in becoming a member of yet another church as so many modern day pagans and heathens seem to be. Like a big bear he roams alone. He is the enemy of orthodoxy and the foe of conformity. He doesn't bow, scrape, kneel or worship. No human on this planet is superior to him.'

I nodded. It was evident that I had witnessed an area that Crow was very deeply passionate about.

'So that's what I mean when I say; a real Odinist. Man, there are so many universalists and racists and cultists and other types out there that call themselves Odinists. In the eyes of the Odin Brotherhood these people are nothing of the sort.'

As he said that my mind flew to the names of several modern-day organizations that, in my estimation, fit the bill of what Crow was saying. I nodded in appreciation of his words.

'Oh, and by the way,' he added. 'When I say "he," I am just using that to illustrate. There are actually women in the Odin Brotherhood so it could easily have been "she."'

I got that. We had discussed it briefly before. I knew, as he did, that in many cases women did not think the Odin Brotherhood was open to them because of the name. This was not so, of course. I had been told once that the name was chosen as a subtle form of misdirection among other things, not to create a barrier to women.

'I have heard that there are women in the Odin Brotherhood,' I said. 'Naturally I don't know what their numbers would be like or the roles they play.'

'There are women in the Brotherhood. I know that for a fact,' he said. 'I think we discussed this before. The Brotherhood was in fact founded by a woman. If you consider The-Power-of-Innocence, the daughter of the widow, there were two females there when the Brotherhood was started. Not only that, but to this day women play an equal part in the tradition.'

'So you have been told,' I said.

'Yes,' he replied. 'I have no reason not to believe it. You know as well as I do that the Brotherhood is open to any who have been called by the Gods and who have the Bloodfire in their veins.'

Bloodfire; I liked that. It was a term coined by my old friend and teacher, Ari, many years ago. It was his way of describing the fierce life energy of a Warrior as it manifested itself in his or her words and deeds. Ari had contended that a person was either gifted with Bloodfire at birth by the Gods or not at all; that only those who possessed it could truly understand its essence and that it was recognizable by others who also had the sacred gift.

I had used the term around Crow and he had loved it. It was good to hear him put it into use.

'That's really all the ground I wanted to cover today,' Crow said suddenly, polishing off his beverage.

I pointed out that we really hadn't been there very long and he assured me that he had nowhere pressing to be that evening.

He did have one request though; that I turn off my recorder for the rest of the time we were sitting there. He said it would be nice not to feel like he was being interviewed for a change.

We had a chuckle at that and indeed I turned off the device. After that our subject matter ranged all over the place - from the mundane to the exotic, though it rarely returned to the subject of the Odin Brotherhood. I had the impression that although the Odin Brotherhood was a very central thing in Crow's life there were times when he wanted simply to blend in as an "ordinary" guy, as he once put it.

We talked for at least a couple of hours in this way and I found it very enjoyable. Eventually the evening crowd started to filter into the pub and things got a little livelier. Someone mentioned that there would soon be a hockey game on the big screen TV near the bar, and we decided we would order something to eat and stay to watch it.

At one point, Crow gestured toward the window and I turned to see what he was pointing at. I grinned as I turned back: the torrential rain had turned into a light falling of snow.

'Typical weather for this time of year,' I said. 'Unpredictable as usual, but you know it's likely going to be wet.'

Crow looked past me out at the gently drifting flakes. They had already begin to accumulate and were covering the vehicles in the parking area with a light, white coating.

'Some things are not predictable though, my friend,' he said. 'That's why we prepare.'

8

Sojourn

Crow sat down at the table across from me and reached into the pack on the ground beside him. He rustled around in there for a moment before pulling a stuffed brown Kraft envelope out and placing it on the table.

'This is for you,' he said. 'But I don't want you to open it until after I'm gone.'

'Feel like telling me what's in it?'

Crow leaned back in his seat. He looked somehow different but I could not place it. His appearance was much as I remembered it from our last, largely social meeting in North Vancouver in October. His hooded pullover was one I had not seen before; brown with spiral patterns on it, but that was not it. I could not place what I sensed was different about him.

'You got that little tape dealy thing of yours?' he asked.

Since I had met him the first time I made a habit of keeping the compact, beat up little recording device with me. I had learned from experience that one could never tell when the enigmatic Crow would show up. I nodded and extracted the device from an outer pocket of my pack.

'I feel like a reporter carrying this thing around, you know,' I said as I set it down and clicked it on.

Crow nodded as he watched the tiny red light come on.

'Helpful for old guys with bad memories, eh?' he asked.

I estimated Crow at being very close in age to me. I did not think there were too many years between us.

'Not likely,' I grinned sarcastically. 'But you use the things that work.'

'I hear ya,' he said.

After a moment Crow motioned to the envelope that sat on the table between us.

'There are stories in there that you might be interested in,' he said. 'They were passed along to me by someone who thought they might help you understand more about the Sojourn.'

'I see,' I said. 'So these are anecdotes of a sort?'

'Well, they are mostly notes. The people who experienced these things are not writers like you are. I think you will be able to make some sense of them when you read them.'

'We have spoken about the Sojourn before,' I said.

'Yes, we have,' he replied. 'But there are two things going on right now; one is that I just got these. I figured you would be interested in seeing what these stories can teach.'

'What's the other thing?'

'What?'

'You said that there were two things going on right now,' I said.

'Oh, yeah,' he said, grinning somewhat sheepishly. 'The second thing is that Solstice is on its way.'

'Care to comment on that?' I asked. I thought I could at least try.

'Well, other than the obvious hint, ah, not really.' He smiled.

I thought as much. I noted that Crow's visits had been increasing in frequency of late. I had actually seen him twice in October though on the second occasion it had been very brief. He had come to ask me about my experience in the coastal mountains and if there were any places I might recommend with a good view of the north. I told him of a few places I knew of, places best attempted in the dry weather of summer.

At first I had wondered about that, though later I suspected he had been making a list of potential places where one might conduct the Sojourn.

'Well, thanks for bringing me this,' I said, gesturing to the envelope. 'I will make good use of it.'

Now it was mid-November. I had been sitting in the café of a college completely unrelated to my university, where I had gone to track down a book I was looking for. How Crow had found me there was a mystery, though his sudden impromptu appearances had long since ceased to amaze me.

'I came to add one tale of my own. That way you will have three to add to your book,' he said. 'I thought a long time about this...whether I could trust you not to reveal too many details about me, but I have noticed that you have been a pretty straight-up guy. You are good for your word.'

'I have kept my promises,' I replied. 'I have not tried to background search you. I haven't tried to follow you and, as I promised, I will erase these tapes when the book is done.'

He nodded. It seemed that this was good enough for him.

'Besides I don't even know who you really are,' I said. 'I will admit I sometimes keep an eye out for you when I am on campus, but beyond that I leave you to your own business.'

'I appreciate that,' he said. 'That's why I will tell you what I am about to tell you. I don't mind if you share this, just keep the details about me to a minimum.'

I told him I had no problem with that.

'The people who gave me the stories in the envelope have the same idea that I do. A person can talk about the Sojourn all they want but the truth is that without actually doing it, it's hard to say what it's really all about. Sometimes teaching or doing is done by example. I know it's the best way I learn, so these stories are basically examples of things surrounding the Sojourn.'

'Are these actual documentation of people's Sojourns?' I asked. I was at first a bit surprised considering the anonymity issues involved, but after a moment's thought I realized that when certain details are left out, secrecy could be preserved.

'Two of them are Sojourns,' he confirmed. 'One is a Calling.'

'The thing that leads a person to do the Sojourn?'

'Yes,' he replied. 'After a person is seen by the Gods as ready they will be given a sign of some kind. In the traditions of the Odin Brotherhood it often comes as a very powerful dream. The dream directs them to do the Sojourn.'

I recalled having a very powerful dream, one that I had experienced twice as a matter of fact. I have described it earlier in this work. However to me the dream was an indication to become

172

more of a seeker in my life. I did not see it as a calling of the sort Crow was talking about.

I looked again at the battered envelope on the table and was very flattered that certain people had chosen to allow me to see their stories, much less allow me to put them in my book. I told Crow this and he smiled.

'I know you are trustworthy,' he said. 'Otherwise we would never have met.'

I nodded my head. There was nothing I felt I could say to that.

'So, let's get to it then,' he said. 'But first....'

He leaned over and pulled his battered thermos out. A few deft moments later there was a steaming cup sitting in front of him. As usual he offered me some but I declined, indicating the empty coffee cup next to me. I had already had two cups of the stuff and was trying to cut down.

When Crow was settled in he took a big hearty sip of his coffee and leaned over slightly and shifted his chair so that his right forearm was on the table.

I smiled and told him that he had a certain Han Solo style to his ways and to that he chuckled and replied that he took that as a compliment.

'Okay, bro,' he said. 'This first one is mine. It's my Calling.'

Many things came into place for me at that moment. I had known that Crow, quite knowledgeable in the ways of the Odin Brotherhood, had been planning to go on the Sojourn for some time. Also from his references to the Solstice over the past year I had an idea that this might be the year he would set out on it. Yet somehow the fact that he had received a Calling, the sacred dream, and was willing to share that with me caused it to somehow become more real.

'Thanks for sharing it with me,' I said.

'No problem,' he said, taking another sip of his coffee. 'I guess I will just start in.'

Crow spent the next twenty minutes or so describing the experience of his calling to me and although I recorded this I ignored the device I had and listened very attentively. I did not want to miss anything in the way of emotional or physical content that might not be picked up by the machine. What follows below is Crow's story as he told it to me.

It was a very real dream - scary real. I could smell things and feel things like the wind on my skin and the dirt on the ground. I was sitting in a camp. I was way out in the woods somewhere, in the mountains somewhere I can't remember being before.

I had a nice little camp set up for myself. There was a nice little fire crackling in the middle and, like I say, I could hear the flames eating through the wood and smell the pine and other bits as they burned. There was a bit of a wind going through the camp and I could tell it was coming up from a valley that was way down below me. I had a view of it through some trees at the edge of my camp. I could smell the trees and the other things you can smell in the forest.

I looked behind me and I saw my tent sitting there. It looked like it could probably hold one or maybe two people in a pinch. It was an old-style A-Frame tent – you know, the kind that has a kind of triangular shape with two poles and a rope holding the front and back tight. The tent looked like it was made of old-style canvas. It was a creamy coffee color. Through the door I could see my sleeping bag lying there all rolled out. It was the sleeping bag I normally use in my campouts, in the waking world.

I noticed that the wind was shifting and for some reason I had the impression it was coming from the north. I also noticed that the sky had changed and was darkening toward sunset.

So in this dream I sat down next to the fire and fed a few sticks in. There seemed to be lots of wood around so I didn't go collecting any.

The dream seemed so real. I could touch and taste and smell everything. I was there.

So after awhile the sky turned orange and then red...and finally purple-black. The stars weren't far behind and within a very short time there were millions of them sparkling in the sky like somebody threw buckets full of white and colored diamonds on a big black velvet canvas.

The wind got a little bit colder too and suddenly I realized that I was wearing my old beat-up green Mackinaw jacket. The jacket was warm enough for this summer night I found myself in.

I kind of lost myself in the dream and believe it or not I started to daydream inside the dream. I snapped out of it after awhile and I realized I was doing that. I also knew it was a dream I was in but I didn't care. I knew that this would be a dream that I would remember. It was a good dream so I just relaxed and went along for the ride.

After awhile it got really black. All around the little circle of light my fire made, the forest went black as coal. You know it always seemed to me that in the forest the night time comes suddenly – like someone flipped a switch and bang: it's dark. So I settled in to watch my fire crackle away.

Until I suddenly felt a presence nearby.

It wasn't one of those things you can really describe. It was not a particular sound or anything but just a kind of instinctive feeling you get when you feel something is slightly out of whack – or someone is watching you.

I knew whatever it was, was somewhere in the north of camp, where there was a fairly large clearing between the trees. I wanted to get up at first but found that I couldn't do that. I felt welded to the ground somehow but rather than get worried I just stayed where I was and looked into the darkness.

After awhile I could see some shapes come out of the darkness – right at the back of the clearing, from the blackness of the trees. At first I couldn't make out what they were but after a bit I could see that they were people. There were eight of them.

As they got closer I could see they were wearing hooded robes of some kind. They had the hoods pulled up so that I couldn't see any faces. At first I thought these robes were black but as they got closer to me I could see in the light of the fire and the rising moon that they were actually dark forest colors – like dark green and brown. They were all really quiet as they came toward me.

Finally they got to about ten feet away and I could see that each one of them had a thong of some kind around their necks. Each one had a silver ring tied on that thong and the rings were all silver. These looked like they were bigger than a finger ring so I assumed they were some kind of amulet or medallion.

They also had in their hands long wooden staffs, kind of like hiking sticks but I had a feeling that maybe they were not just used for balance when walking up trails.

For some reason, maybe it was body language, maybe it was instinct, I knew that half of them were women and the other half, men.

About six feet away they all stopped and they were standing in a kind of half-circle formation facing me at my fire. One of them raised a hand in a kind of greeting gesture. I could tell that she was one of the leaders of the group.

There was this feeling of intense calm going through me at the time, but at the same time my instincts were telling me that these people were very special and they were not ordinary people.

Suddenly my mind started buzzing and I started thinking about the Odin Brotherhood and what they have said about being visited here in Midgard by the Gods and Goddesses. Then my sense of humour suddenly kicked in and I thought to myself, 'Here I am sitting in front of a bunch of Old Ones and I didn't even dress nice.'

Suddenly, after that thought I had the feeling that my body had somehow been released. It was like I was now able to get up as I had wanted to do the minute I had sensed the disturbance by the trees.

So I got up and stretched my legs for a second. I stood there for a minute looking at them. They were very quiet and said nothing. They just stood there looking at me.

It wasn't long after that, that I felt another presence and sure enough someone else emerged from the trees and came up behind the ones that were already standing there. They moved aside in the middle of their little half-circle to let him come through. I had no doubt they had been expecting him.

This ninth one was a bit larger than the other ones and as he came up to the fire I could see the bristles of a full grey beard sticking out from underneath his hood. He was a powerful person, I could somehow tell, but I sensed no trouble coming from him.

This man came up much closer than the others had and when he was about three feet away he suddenly dipped his staff down toward my fire. It was then that I realized it wasn't just a staff either but a spear with a long, silver tip. A second later he raised the spear back up so the tip pointed at the sky.

I was watching him closely but then he moved so fast I could hardly believe it. In one movement he levelled the spear at me and thrust the tip before me. It happened so fast I knew that if he had wanted to hurt me I would have had a hole in me.

But that's not what happened. Instead the spear tip stopped just at the surface of my skin. It went right under the coat and my shirt and for a second I felt a kind of freezing-burning sensation. It all happened so quickly because the next thing I know the spear was pulled away and the man was standing there in front of me again, pointing the tip back to the sky.

For a minute it was all silent around there. The only sound you could hear was the crackling of the fire and the wind in the tree tops.

Then the man with the spear said one word to me: 'Continue.'

After a second he nodded at me and turned to go back into the forest. The rest of his band followed him and in a minute more they were all gone.

I remember standing there by the fire, amazed by all of this that had happened. After a second I unbuttoned my jacket and coat to see if any mark had been made on me by that spear.

Sure enough there was: It was thick and black. It looked kind of like an upside down letter 'V' and it also looked like a cross between a tattoo or a burn, but it didn't feel like either. I remember thinking it also looked a bit like an inverted chevron.

As I stood there in the firelight looking at the upper part of my left chest, the mark started to fade. After a minute or so it was like it had completely dissolved into my skin. It was gone.

I sat down again at my fire. I didn't know what else to do.

And that is what I remember of the dream. What I do remember though was that after I woke up the next day I had a powerful burning feeling in the exact spot where the mark had been placed. I think it was there to make sure I remembered the dream, and I had no problem with that. The dream is still really clear in my head, as if it was not a dream but a normal memory.

I sat for a moment in silence. I wanted to be sure he was finished telling me his tale. He had and I thanked him for sharing his amazing experience.

He seemed a little bit unsettled at having told me the tale, as if there was still a tiny part of him that was unsure as to whether he had done the right thing or not.

After a moment more he settled back, finished off his coffee and screwed the lid back on. I had the impression that he would soon decide to leave.

'The Calling is a powerful thing,' he said. 'Everybody supposedly has a different experience but I have also heard that there are some instances where people have had similar dreams. Either way it was a very heavy thing as far as I am concerned. It was so real it was like you and me sitting here. I don't think I will ever forget it.'

'Again I would like to thank you for sharing it with me,' I said.

With that, Crow got up from his seat and placed his thermos

back in his pack. A second after that he shouldered his bag. It was obvious he was going to leave.

'Keep those pages in there safe,' he said, gesturing to the envelope on the table. 'I hope they are of use to you.'

'I have no doubt that they will be,' I replied.

'Okay, I am going to take off,' he said. 'Have fun with the goodies.'

'I guess I'll see you around,' I said by way of a farewell.

'You probably will,' he said good-naturedly, and left.

I sat for a moment and watched him walk away, up the stairs and then disappear into the streets. Then I opened the envelope before me and looked through the papers that had been inside. Both were printed on standard 8.5 x 11 inch white paper though one looked like it had been produced by a computer printer. The other one looked as if it had been produced by an old fashioned typewriter.

The two documents had very obviously been penned by two very different people and as I read through them both I knew that Crow had been right: they were both good examples of the form a Sojourn could take. They were also good examples of what Crow had said with regard to the improvisational skills expected in an Odinist: the two others who had shared their experiences exhibited this fierce determination and adaptability quite well.

Crow was also right at least in the case of one document: it was obviously a typed transcription of someone's notes, detailed as they were. The second document was penned by a more sophisticated hand. Regardless of penmanship, I was very happy to have both.

I took the documents home with me that night and looked over them some more before I finally started to translate them into a book-useable form.

What follows are the two documents I was given. I have edited them as minimally as possible and presented them as accurately as I can. Additionally, the titles of each are as they were presented to me in the original documents. I have no further information as to the meaning or origin of these names.

#1: The Tale of Dust-Legs

I completed my journey to the Odin Brotherhood three years ago. It was not the experience I expected it to be, yet I am reminded that it is the way of the Gods to be mysterious at times.

I would say also that I am a pagan of many years experience. I began my life as many do, in a family that in ignorance walked a Christian path that profited us little.

Eventually though, frustration and curiosity drove/lured me away from such wasteful ways and set me on a path of discovery that led me first to witchcraft and then Indian spirituality and finally to what modern men call Asatru.

Ultimately though, after years in practice, I found that Asatru was not sufficient to meet my spiritual needs. I found that many people were simply not deep enough there and it seemed that there were too many in that tradition who did not think as I did, and so I moved on.

After years of searching I came upon that interesting little book about the Odin Brotherhood. I read it eagerly as I had always been keenly interested in such things as mysterious orders and secret societies. The author intrigued me – so much so that I set out on a quest to learn more. This was not as easy as I had at first imagined, as the Odin Brotherhood proved true to its secret ways.

Eventually though, I found connections that allowed me to dig deeper. What I discovered was that there are great and profound truths in the teachings of the Odin Brotherhood. I also discovered that again the Odin Brotherhood speaks true when they say that their ways are not for everyone: there are things I will not speak of in detail here, but I will say that I am convinced that the Odin Brotherhood is not for everyone.

As a matter of fact what I learned gave me pause when I had thoughts of possibly joining the Odin Brotherhood. I wondered if I was worthy, even though I had honored the old Gods for a very long time.

I set ideas of Sojourning aside and focused my attention on studying as much of the lore as I could. I learned many things.

Then one evening, at least two years after I had first read the Odin Brotherhood book, I was astonished by an extremely powerful and real-seeming dream that shook the foundations of my world. I will not go into the details of the dream but it was a potent and poignant awakening for me.

After the dream I began to think again about embarking on the Sojourn. It was not long before I decided that the time was right: I set my sights upon the upcoming winter solstice.

I readied myself for my adventure by reviewing and re-reading all that I could about the Odin Brotherhood. I also re-read as many of the Sagas and Eddas that I could; especially the tales of the Codex Regius.

Finally the time of the solstice was rapidly approaching. I had a location in mind up in the mountains and I prepared my supplies for the potentially treacherous journey.

My wife had graciously made me a beautiful white robe of pure linen for the journey as well. All she had known was that I was planning to go on a meditative retreat in the hills. I had requested only material for a wrap or a shroud but she decided that such would not do. I was happy with the long sleeved, hooded garment. It had been tailored for me with love and I did not think the Gods would mind.

As well, I would say also that I had managed to make the acquaintance of a mysterious person from the Odin Brotherhood during the preceding year. This person, who I had never personally met but with whom I had only correspondences by mail and internet, had emphasized to me that it was largely the initiative of the neophyte that was appreciated by the order. He told me that there were only certain things that must be seen to and he instructed me in those.

My sacred knife was of my own inspiration. Long ago I had

been gifted with a very sharp blade that despite its age carried an edge like it had just come from the shop it was made in. The blade has deep significance to me. It was not the kind of blade that I ordinarily would use for mundane tasks, but rather I had long made use of it in more sacred ways. I thought it would be perfect for the Sojourn.

The lightning-wood had at first proved elusive: I spent months looking for evidence of lightning-struck trees, yet I had been unsuccessful in gathering any for my ritual. Finally, only a month before December I happened to be on a walking trip through a deep area of cedar forest and I found the remains of several lightning-killed trees, including birch and holly.

I left offerings to the Vaettir and took what wood I thought I would need.

Finally the solstice was almost upon us. I explained to my wife the rough location that I was venturing into; this to ease her mind though she knows I am a man of many years' wilderness experience. She is a strong pagan woman and with that she wished me well on my journey.

I took food and drink in my pack, as well as survival materials so that I would not endanger myself needlessly. I also took a bottle of good ale and a copy of the Hávamál.

I had wrapped one more item in my gear and that was my long sword 'Taufr', enclosed in a thin blanket and strapped across the frame of my pack. I did not want any undue attention by sheeplings or mundane folks. I was not bringing my blade to gain notice but rather because such an implement is the tool of the warrior. As a result Taufr was concealed until such a time as I was deep in the bush.

The journey was not an easy one. I made my way off the roads and ventured deep into the bush. Interestingly enough the winter had been an unseasonably warm one and rather than finding deep snow at the location I had chosen, I found but small patches of it. I had been disappointed because I had wanted to venture even higher up, yet there were telltale signs among those treacherous peaks that avalanches could easily occur. I did not wish to make my beautiful blonde-haired pagan wife a widow and so I accepted my destiny in that little place amongst the pines.

The place I had chosen faced northwest and through the trees I could catch glimpses of the sea that surged on rocks far below.

It rained quite frequently and I was glad that I had brought a small portable tent for shelter and a serviceable blanket and sleeping bag with me.

I settled into my small camp one day before the Sojourn cycle was to begin, and so I enjoyed myself in the quiet solitude of those dark woods. Small animals came to visit me but nothing larger than a rabbit ever came to call during that time.

The next day I began the fast. As I had no ice or snow for the purposes of the ritual I had substituted cold creek water. It had not long ago been snow, high in the inaccessible peaks above me.

Many of us are spoiled and fat in today's society. I was reminded of this as my body began to demand nourishment even though I consider myself to be in fairly good condition. Fasting is not easy but with determination and a relaxed attitude many things can be achieved.

On the second day, the first day of the actual fast, something unprecedented happened. In retrospect it reinforced the lesson that the Odinist must be ever prepared and ever ready to improvise.

I had a growing feeling that there was someone coming close to my encampment. I could not see or hear anyone, but the feeling of an impending human presence continued to nag at me. I had taken care to be a good distance from the trail and I had made sure there was little evidence of my passing, yet there was that feeling.

Finally I gave in to the feeling and hastily pulled apart my tiny camp. I extinguished my small fire and did as much as I could to erase any evidence that I had been there.

I had little choice then, but to leave the area and try to make my way to another place where I could complete my task. I walked for what seemed like hours seeking a place that felt special. Once or twice I thought I had found a spot only to experience that same earlier feeling that said 'don't do this because you will be disturbed.'

I did not understand the feeling: I was far from the trails used by local people and in the dead of winter it was even more unlikely that I would meet anyone. Yet the voice inside was deep and strong. I treated it as the voice of instinct and obeyed it.

Throughout my wet and cold quest through the woods I had not seen or heard anyone, yet the inner voice had been something I could not ignore. Regardless I was glad that I had complied with its warnings.

It was many hours later and rapidly approaching dusk of the first day when I finally found a place that I thought was suitable. It was further down-slope on the mountainside and somewhat closer to the sea as I could now hear the waves crashing below. Yet despite this it felt as though it was a place in which I would be certain to be undisturbed.

I hastily settled in for the night with a loudly complaining stomach that bread would not cure.

The third day, or the second day of the Sojourn fast, was misery. The mind wanders. Even though I have experience in meditation, in meditation one can easily dismiss distractions. When one's own body is causing the distraction it is much more difficult to master.

The urge to give in and eat something from my pack was great. As well the urge to simply get up and return to civilization gnawed at the back of my conscious mind.

I ignored these things after considerable effort.

Eventually I embraced the potential of the night. I sang softly around my fire and within a time, went to my bed.

Finally the sacred day had arrived. I spent the day hungry, as I had decided to hold off on the remainder of the bread I had in my supply. I wanted my head to be clear and indeed, I wanted to have the extra stash of food handy after the ritual, just in case I might have need of it for the trip home.

Morning melded into afternoon and though the day seemed long, even on one of the shortest days of the year, eventually it faded to twilight and then darkness. I sat for what seemed like hours around that tiny fire I had there. I waited for the time when I would perform the rite.

I had reached an inner state of calm despite my angry stomach and had learned to re-focus my senses acutely on the surrounding landscape. I tried to take in everything I could and I sat doing this for what seemed like hours.

After I had done that I began a meditation. I pondered the Hávamál and the wisdom of Har in that blackened little clearing so far from my home.

At about ten in the evening I allowed my tiny fire to go out on its own. I wanted the makeshift fire pit to be cleared before I built the sacred fire in it. Watching the little fire break apart to embers and then to ashes darkening in the chill air was like saying farewell to a friend.

I sat for awhile in the cold darkness and prepared myself. I set out my blade and I removed my shroud from the backpack. I prepared my sacred wood.

Not long after that I removed my sweater and shirt and packed them away in my bag. Bare chested, yet still wearing my trousers and boots, I donned the soft white robe that my love had made for me. In the act of donning the robe I felt somehow transformed and I realized what an old Sorcerer friend of mine had said many years ago was true: 'Appropriate garb can trigger a transformation in consciousness for ritual.'

I then felt the urge to draw my sword near. It was as though

Taufr was upset at having little part to play in my adventure as yet. She wanted to be free.

And so I unsheathed her and held her aloft, all two and a half feet of gleaming, razor sharp, moon-silver. She seemed to almost bask in the brilliant starlight between cracks in the anvil grey cloud cover. Now she was happy.

I stood for a moment in the intensity of the dark and listened: the sounds of the night had earlier been many but now all I could hear was the hiss of the wind and the surge of the sea below. After a moment I sat down again, warrior-style with my legs crossed and my blade across my knees. I remember thinking lustfully that tonight would see some blood shedding in a powerful way.

That was when I heard the voice.

The voice was loud and insistent. It was a voice that at first startled me and saw me snatching up my blade in a defensive way. It took me several seconds to realize that the voice had not been an outer phenomenon, heard by the ears, but a kind of inner phenomenon; heard and understood by the brain and perhaps even more importantly, the spirit.

The voice had an uncanny quality to it: There was a high pitched sound underlying it that sounded like the buzz of a tiny insect. It was almost like a carrier-wave of some kind.

This voice was more potent than the inner voice that had warned me to vacate my earlier place and it said one thing very clearly:

'You must go to the sea.'

I hesitated. It was pitch dark and I was on terrain that while I was roughly familiar with it, I was not in the area that I had originally planned to camp. The mountains are treacherous enough in the daytime and especially in the winter. The same mountains in the night were at least triply dangerous places to go off trail.

'You must go to the sea.'

The voice repeated itself. There was then no mistake that it had been really heard the first time. Here was no fast-induced figment of the imagination, but something deeply instinctive. It was a voice that sounded male and my soul reflexively surged towards what it was saying – as though I was being given advice by a very close and loved kinsman.

'You must go to the sea.'

I looked at my watch. I had less than two hours until midnight. My logical mind immediately rebelled at the craziness of the thought that was brewing in my head; that I would accept the challenge and plunge headlong in the darkness to seek the sea – though it might result in a headlong plunge from a cliff or some other unpleasant surprise.

I fought off the conflicting thoughts and strove to think clearly; to work out my plan in a focused, rational way. I was unsuccessful in this. I realized that I was experiencing a central tenet of the Odin Brotherhood: the warrior trusts his guts and plunges in – he embraces the fire of destiny when it is held before him. The warrior does not shy away; he lives.

'I shall do it!' I exclaimed in as fierce and throaty manner as I could.

Suddenly, as though I had been heard – and I am sure that I was, the high pitched whine, that sound that had accompanied the voice, stopped. I was again bathed in the ambient sounds of the woods.

I threw caution and logical thought to the wind and packed my reason into a small compartment in the back of my mind. I had made my choice and by the Gods I would see it through. If I was to perish then it would be a glorious, natural death. Far better than the fate of many in this day and age.

I was back on my feet.

'Apologies, little sister,' I said hastily to Taufr, and placed her back in her sheath. The scabbard was still strapped to my pack-frame so I did not have to re-attach it for transport.

I packed my gear with the help of a flashlight I had brought with me, and was quickly ready to depart.

But depart to where? How would I accomplish this?

I left it up to the ones who had guided me. I left it up to the ones who had told me to go to the sea.

I stood for a moment in the chill of near-absolute blackness. There was only the song of the breeze, the distant surge of surf and the slight scent of smoke left over from my now dead fire.

I shifted my pack into balance on my back but left the hip strap unbuckled. I had a feeling that the journey may necessitate a sudden jettison of my gear if disaster struck.

I lowered my arms somewhat to my sides and, palms open facing forward, I let myself go.

Suddenly there was a breeze. I call it that because it is the only word I can think of to describe it. It was cooler than the ambient and it kind of drew me toward it. I hesitated only for a moment before saying 'Guide me.' To the surrounding night.

A certain direction felt best in light of the strange breeze-like sensation I was feeling. I went in the direction of least resistance and before long I came upon a tiny trail cut through the trees that I had not seen before. I suspected that it was a game trail rather than a man-made one. It traveled downhill on a very steep angle.

Flashlight in one hand and the other to help guide my way I plunged into the uncertain dark, trusting the Sacred Ones would guide me to where I needed to be.

The Journey was largely a blur. It had been a maelstrom of whipping branches and the dodging over rocks and slippery roots along the ever steepening path. Many times I had thought it certain that the yawning emptiness of a cliff's edge would appear directly before me, yet each time this happened I was presented with a short drop to another level and more scrambling.

I felt as though I was on some kind of auto-pilot; that I was allowing my deeper animal instinct to guide me rather than my years-honed trail smarts and common sense.

I knew I could easily be killed, yet for the strangest reason this thought created an odd, fierce glow in my heart and for a second I saw myself seated at a table full of Warriors with Odin himself at the head. In the fleeting vision Odin gestured towards me and gave me praise for my audacity.

Suddenly the trail steepened even more: the tree-line broke and I paused for a second to take in the glory before me. Below and beyond the wild silver vastness of the sound stretched toward the Northwest. The sea: Aegir's realm. Above and over a darkened forest point of land the steel grey of the cloud cover had shattered into ever-widening cracks and from behind them a silver moon glowed argent light across the water.

I took in the fresh invigorating air during my short pause. It fired my blood and I thought about what an American Indian friend of mine had called that kind of air: 'A spirit-breeze.'

I set back to my journey and walked to the edge of the short trail I found before me. Again I became wary that a cliff might lurk there but upon examination I saw that while it was nearly a cliff, it had roots and various outcroppings that would serve as handholds on the way down.

I scrambled down the steep landscape and again found myself on a rough, rubble-strewn trail. The wall of forest again loomed blackly yet strangely inviting before me. I could hear the sea, now much louder than before.

I plunged forward.

Eventually I broke through the forest cover, some hour or more after I had set out. I stood some hundred feet above the beach on an outcropping of grey worn stone and again beheld the majesty of the sea. A fierce wind had begin to blow in from the Northwest and it was only then that I realized I had worn my sacred white robe, open at the front, all the way down the mountainside.

189

Much to my surprise the robe was still gleaming white. It had barely seen the passage of the trails in its pale fabric and for that I was thankful.

I scrambled down the short cliff face and soon I stood on a pebble-coated grey sand beach facing the sea. The salt air lashed my face and as the wind picked up the waves began breaking in huge explosions against the tidal rocks in the surf.

I stopped again for a moment to take in the raw spectacle: not a single sign of human civilization could be seen. Not even a light on the other side of the sound denoting a human habitation or road – not even the lights of a plane in the sky. It was as though I had stepped back a thousand years into a better time.

I looked at my watch again. I had less than 30 minutes to prepare for the ritual.

I placed my pack somewhat back in the rocks and hastily set up my tent in a small, grassy area that stood above the tide-line. I stowed my gear and unstrapped Taufr's scabbard from the pack-frame. I belted the sword belt and for a moment more, stood there, clad in my flowing windswept robe, sword at hip, facing the sea.

I wore but one adornment and that was an old ring made of red stone and carved with Frejya's Aett – a protective talisman – on a leather thong around my neck. In another tradition this is called a Lore-Stone. I had carved it myself years ago. It had been stained with my blood. I felt like it tingled in the air and that it, like my sword, was happy to be unleashed in the purity of the night.

I felt that even though I had been fasting my body surged with life and energy. I thought of the ancient rune Sowilo and imagined that the energy was far beyond what adrenalin could provide: it was a gift of the Gods.

I forced myself to back away from marveling at the scene and set to the creation of my sacred fire.

It did not take long to prepare the small stone ring and set the sacred lightning wood in place.

Finally I sat in the warrior-style on the beach, Taufr across my knees and gazed upon the scene before me once more. I drank it all in and as I did I saw myself as but a single, gleaming Warrior-star in a vast cascading multiverse of other stars.

I felt at home.

I looked at my watch one more time before taking it off and putting it away. The time was rapidly approaching.

I started the sacred fire and there was no difficulty as the dried wood took to flame in a swirling, upward dance of yellow and orange sparkling light.

I took that moment to quickly strip to the waist, take off my sword and wade nearly waist deep into the surging, near freezing sea. I had not had the opportunity to partake of the pure-water bath as a part of my rite and so I asked Aegir, Njord and the Lady Ran if they might accommodate me. I splashed myself liberally with the icy water and after a moment of basking with savage delight returned to the beach where I re-donned my robe and sword.

I sat and prepared myself mentally. I rehearsed the oath and the names of the Gods and Goddesses who I would soon be addressing. I could almost feel the presence of certain someone's beginning to close in on me from many angles. I felt as though I was being watched.

I exalted in it.

At last the time came.

I stood before the blazing fire. My sacred blade was finally withdrawn from its sheath.

'In the name of Violence, necessary violence!' I announced, beginning the ritual.

Blood flowed from three diagonal slashes across my chest. The blood flowed freely.

I spoke the sacred words, intoning them with as much power as I could bring to the experience. Waves crashed in the rocks around me and the free wind surged.

The blade kissed the flames and more words were spoken.

Finally the final loud utterance: 'The rite is finished. Let my violent thrust into the future begin!'

I stood there for long moments before I extinguished the fire, blood flowing and spirit soaring.

Finally, respectfully, I placed sand and water on the flames, reducing them to darkness.

I stood again for a moment in the embrace of the howling sea wind.

'I did as you asked' I shouted above the roar. 'I came to the sea.'

To my surprise...or perhaps I should not have been, the voice returned.

'You will find that some of the remaining fears you have in your heart have been forever removed.'

I stood there, stunned, absorbing the words for they had been as real as if there was a man standing right next to me, speaking them.

I offered thanks to the wind.

The voice spoke again.

'Here is wisdom: The ones from the desert will turn this entire world into a desert if they are not stopped. Be a part of the force that stops them. Spread the lore.'

And I stood there again for long moments, waiting for more.

There was nothing else said to me in that fashion.

I unsheathed Taufr and saluted the Gods and my people; my true people who are all tribal in their hearts and who know the Old Ways. I saluted those-who-know, who were now my brothers and sisters. My oath had bound me to them as well as to the Gods as far as I was concerned. My loyalty was absolute.

I felt intense and root-deep pride surging through my veins as I stood there in that lonely yet never alone place. I had crossed a line that few would ever dare to.

I thought about that sacred Lady; the Shrouded-One-of-Odin. I thought about her brave children and I thought about all those who over the centuries have striven that I might stand upon a lonely strand in the midst of a rising sea-storm.

I felt a connection to all of them, I had become part of the lineage; part of the line of the world-changing elite.

I felt so far above the herd. I felt truly indomitable.

I re-sheathed my sword, wiped clean my sacred blade and set to creating a comfortable camp for myself. I built a new fire away from the first one and there I offered libation to my older kin as I feasted upon the food and drink that I had saved for this time.

I had been created again as an implement of the Gods and I knew I would endeavor to hone that weapon razor sharp.

I had been given the knowledge to be truly free.

I had been given the tools to be truly alive.

I am Dust-Legs.

I share my story with you who-would-know.

#2 The Tale of Shield-Maiden

I have always had visions and dreams. As I grew older I heard the voices of the Old Ones, they who are sometimes called Gods and Goddesses. They spoke to me in whispers, in waking visions and dreams of other worlds.

I chose a pagan path at a fairly early age but it was many years before I really understood it was the Old Ones of the Vanir who called to me strongly. From them I learned to walk the wending ways.

I also learned of the Odin Brotherhood. I knew none who claimed to be of the Brotherhood, but when I read the book I knew immediately that these were ones who knew the truth which so many lesser humans feared. They knew that the Old Ones are alive and among us. They understood the power of dreams and the magic of women who walk between the worlds.

My Calling-dream was totally unexpected and came in the form of a challenge. It came to me early one morning after a night of a long and intense dream of battle. In this dream I was fighting an opponent whose skills equally matched mine. We traded knife-blow for knife-blow, until at last he blinded me by plunging a blade deep into my left eye. I dealt him a killing blow as well and with the last of my strength managed to drag myself into a little copse of trees. I knew I was dying but I was determined to die on my own terms, near the trees.

I had never died in a dream before. But the leaves were green above me and the trees were strong around me and I felt victorious in death.

As the leaves faded from my vision I saw him. His battered hat was pulled low over his face. His beard was white.

He smiled at me and told me I fought a good battle, that it was an important dream. I did not give in. I did not kneel. I knew I could control my own destiny in the dream. I produced weapons. I fought. I was not a victim. And in the end I died well and honorably.

I am exhausted but still in the dreaming. I went to a sacred place to heal. I entered the stone circle and there was a spiral cut into the earth, circling around. I struggled but I managed to reach the center, where I laid down to rest.

The ground opened up beneath me and I fell downwards into the earth, into an underground hall. Before me sat a man dressed in furs, with gray hair.

He stood up. 'Do you know who I am?'

'No.'

'I am Heimdall.'

I was really feeling at a disadvantage. I was exhausted and in pain and I wanted only to rest.

'You want something from me.'

'I do?'

'You want a gift from me.' He showed me words...writing...books.

'You want to write a book: your book to change the world.' It was like he had it, there in his hand, and he could just give it to me.

'Yeah, I do.'

'What do you offer me in return?'

'I'll use my talent, my skills to bring the words to people who need them. I'll write about pagans.'

He laughed. 'How is that a gift to me? Sounds like more of the gift to you.'

What else did I have to offer? My mind raced and for some reason I said, 'I'll make you a cloak.'

'A cloak? Do I need a cloak?'

I shrugged.

Then he laughed. 'Make me a cloak. Sing me a cloak into being. Sing me a cloak of white deerskin. Six white deerskins.' Again a laugh. 'No hurry. When I have my cloak, you will get your book.'

He tossed me a staff and I caught it. 'This will help you,' he said. 'Rest now, and heal. Take your time. Learn more about the Lore.'

It took almost a year for me to learn the lessons I needed to learn, in visions and through dreaming. After each lesson I would be given a white deerskin, until at last I had enough for a cloak for Heimdall. It took a few more months before I finally saw him again in a dream and I presented him with the white cloak. And it was then I knew I was ready to attempt the Sojourn.

I chose the Winter Solstice because I felt I would have a hard time finding the solitude necessary in the summer. Winter is cold and bleak here and I knew there would not be many who would want to spend time outdoors as the sun moved towards the darkest days of the year.

I had a hard time choosing the correct location. I made some plans and they kept falling through. I wondered at first if this was a sign that I should not sojourn, but decided I had just not found the spot that would please the Old Ones.

I procured a white garment. The lightning-struck wood was more difficult since the time of storms was past, but at last I found a great oak that showed signs of storm-fire from earlier in the year. I searched quite a while before locating a blade I felt was fine enough and sharp enough — the tip of one's finger is a very small target.

I told friends and family I was going on a little retreat to write, which was partially true. A few days before the Solstice I traveled to the location I had finally chosen and settled in with my simple food, fresh water and ice, and a couple of notebooks. I wanted no outside distractions to my thoughts — no music or even books.

The place I had chosen could not be considered wilderness, and I had at first discounted it as a proper place for the sojourn. It was, however, isolated. It would not leave my mind. I kept seeing its features. This place had an unusual aura about it, not of bleak and untamed nature but of being a place dedicated to the Old Ones. As Solstice approached I began to accept that this was the place the Old Ones had chosen for me.

The first day was mellow and very quiet. It is not often we are completely alone with our thoughts and I found my mind wandering down interesting paths. I was eating very small amounts and chewing ice and by the second day I was beginning to get very hungry and lightheaded.

The space around me took on a dreamy quality. I felt the Old Ones were very close. As it got dark I had only candlelight and I found myself drifting in and out of visions.

Heimdall appeared before me again, wearing the white deerskin cloak. His face was forbidding as he asked me, 'Why do you want to do this?'

I weighed my words carefully before I spoke. 'I see the changes which are coming. The gates are opening. The Old Ones are returning. I want to stand at the side of the Old Ones and do everything I can to help them. I want to help return the Balance to this world.'

Heimdall seemed pleased at my answer. He smiled and banged his staff on the ground a few times before moving away.

Others came to take his place. Some I recognized. Some I didn't. Few chose to utter their names. All questioned me and I answered them as best I could.

At last the vision faded and I was alone again. The candle had gone out and I lay there in darkness for a time before another vision approached.

I saw only a form draped in a hooded robe, but I knew at once who she was. It was the Shrouded One.

Her anger was almost palpable. I could not see her face but I sensed a wild, deep beauty about her.

'The time has come,' she said, and her voice was shaking with fury. 'At long last, the pendulum swings back. Those of the desert sought to destroy my people and my kind. They should have known it was impossible to wipe us out. As long as one of us still lives, the Old Ways will never die.'

'They say they are merciful. Were they merciful to me as they watched me burn alive? By their mercy they will be destroyed. And I will show them no mercy. The followers of the desert god will die in waves. The earth will drink their blood and be healed. They will be destroyed by the very forces of nature they think they have mastered.'

Her voice was so loud it filled my head until she was no longer speaking to me but through me. Her voice called forth those who slumbered and those who know, for the tide of Solstice had turned and the gates were open. She called forth the Old Ones and spoke to all who would hear her.

I traveled a sleep full of wild dreams that night. In the morning I awoke and went to the sacred grove where I would perform the final ritual and align myself with the Old Ones.

It was damp and rainy but not particularly cold as I circled the grove, getting a sense of the space before I began. It was quiet...very quiet. The place I had chosen seemed to vibrate with expectation.

I lit a tiny fire with the wood I had brought. All around me there was a rustle of wings as birds flew out of the woods to join me, sitting in the trees which ringed the circle.

I stood up but I could not remain still. I paced the grove as I declared, 'In the name of violence...necessary violence!'

I drew the fine blade I had selected. With care I made three incisions in the tip of my index finger until the blade was stained with my blood. This I passed through the flames, watching the blood darken and dry on the blade as I made oath to the Old Ones who live.

I circled the grove again as I named the Old Ones, the words singing and hissing through the drizzle. I felt a fierce and wild joy within me. I felt the joy of the Old Ones as I stepped beyond the mundane and joined those who know.

I poured some of the ice-water on the flames and watched the smoke grow thin. Once again I walked and spoke the words which closed the ceremony, 'The rite is finished. Let my violent thrust into the future begin!'

9

A Warrior's Journey

The Odin Brotherhood speaks often of cycles and circles, both in time and nature. Indeed I had also noticed a certain cyclical nature in my relationship with the enigmatic Crow.

The Odin Brotherhood delves deep into the realm of mystery and as such, as a student of theirs, I could see that Crow was very much already walking in such a way. I began looking for patterns in his behavior and was not entirely surprised to see that especially in the early months of our time together he had always appeared on a day (or night) which had a new moon. I was not sure if this was random chance or not but I did not think so. Crow also preferred to appear in the evenings, though this was not always so.

I had also noticed that with Crow, things often happened in multiples of three or nine. When we were on our forest campout he had brought nine bottles of ale with him. During a rather informal talk about the Gods (which I have not included in this book because it covered much that is already covered in Dr. Mirabello's work) I noted that he only spoke about nine of them.

And so I was pondering these kinds of things as I made my way through the busy crowds at the large bus and train terminal we have near the center of the city. It appeared to me that Crow seemed always to have a method and a reason for everything he did. There were often riddles hidden in his words and I know for a fact that many of them have yet to be solved by me.

The text message had appeared in the morning as I sat having a cup of coffee. Interestingly enough, the message appeared at precisely 9am.

It said: 'Going on a trip. Leaving at 3 today. If you want to see me off meet me where the baby trains fly over their big brothers.'

The message was not all that difficult to decipher since I easily deduced the location he was talking about. Vancouver has a large train and bus terminal near the city core, as I have mentioned. Right next to this station is an elevated track where much smaller commuter trains make their way high above the older station.

I also think that Crow did not wish to be overly cryptic: I think he had genuinely developed a fondness for me as I had for him and he was looking forward to a visit.

As I set out I made a note of the date. It was December 15th.

The station was quite crowded when I arrived in the bright sun of a clear, clean day. A cold breeze blew down from the mountains and people bustled back and forth clutching shopping bags, backpacks and suitcases. The festive season was in full swing and I assumed that many were going to be boarding buses and trains to go visit their loved ones.

I wondered where Crow was going. I also wondered what he would have to say to me when we met. What would he have to add to all of the things he had already passed on to me?

I did not have long to wait for answers. After entering the terminal I saw Crow leaning up against a pillar near a small coffee outlet. He waved me over and I made my way through the push of people to where he stood.

He had a second cup of coffee, steaming in its paper cup, ready for me when I got there. How he had known that I would arrive when I did, around 2 in the afternoon, I had no idea.

I gratefully accepted the coffee. I had not had a cup yet and the chill outside made the warm beverage all the more comforting.

Crow was dressed in the same dark hooded pullover that he had worn when I first met him. He also wore a thick, black down vest over that, along with heavy black cargo style pants and high hiking boots. Settled against the pillar he leaned on was a large expedition-style frame pack in black and brown.

Otherwise he was exactly as he was the last time I had seen him; sporting that wry grin and appearing as casual and relaxed as a coyote who had just eaten a bird.

'You look like you are going on a trip,' I said, in greeting.

'Looks like that doesn't it?' he said. 'I wanted to see you one last time so I could tell you in person that I have enjoyed our talks and all the rest. It felt good to share what I know with somebody who will write it all down.'

'It's my pleasure to help out,' I replied. 'But I will benefit from this as much as you when it gets published. You like to tell me about your adventures and such and I like to write. Good combination.'

There seemed to be a hint of finality in what Crow had said and I wondered if he was finished with our talks together. I thought that there was a lot more about the Odin Brotherhood that I did not yet know, and that what I did know barely skimmed the surface.

'It's getting pretty nippy in the air. I think we might get a bit of snow down here soon,' he commented.

I had to agree. It had almost smelled like snow outside, yet there were no clouds in sight from horizon to horizon.

'I think I have given you a lot of stuff for your book, buddy,' he said, looking at his watch. I had never noticed him wearing a watch before. It was a Breitling; a very nice quality Swiss watch.

'Nice timepiece you have there,' I commented.

'Oh this?' he said. 'It was a gift. You know as in "a gift demands a gift?"'

I nodded. Indeed I was well aware of that natural rule.

'I gotta go soon,' he said. 'Got a fair bit of work ahead of me and I better get to it. I just wanted to say hey before I took off...and to wish you a merry Yule-tide.'

He put out his hand and placed a small tissue wrapped object in my hand.

'Happy Solstice,' he said.

I opened the little package and saw that it contained a single piece of grey, rectangular stone carved with a single Nordic rune: Othala, the rune of homelands, freedom and prosperity.

'Thanks, man,' I said. 'I wish I had something to reciprocate with.'

'You will,' he said brightly. 'Soon you will have done a service for those-who-know everywhere. Soon you will get your book finished. I will buy a copy.'

'When that time comes I will give you a copy,' I said.

He smiled back. 'I hope you get it published, bro. It will do a lot of good and it will help a lot of people find their way back to the Old Ways.'

'That's my hope,' I replied. 'I had a question for you though. One last one before you go on your trip.'

'Shoot,' he replied.

'Readers might want to know this, especially those who feel themselves drawn to the Sojourn. You may not even know this because you are not a member of the Odin Brotherhood yet.'

I paused for a moment, then; 'How should a person go about learning more about the Brotherhood, assuming they want to dig deeper? Assuming I wanted to dig even deeper?'

Crow smiled at the last part of what I had said, but didn't refer to it. 'I will tell you two things to answer your question. The first one is a piece of wisdom that someone gave me. He said, "A person may teach without revealing." I'll leave you to think about that one.'

'The second part?' I asked.

'The second part,' he said, 'is that from what I know those people who complete the Sojourn have ways of making that fact known. There are certain code words or ways of framing things that members of the Odin Brotherhood might use to recognize each other. In the old days, of course, these things were taught from person to person so the signs and symbols got transferred over that way. Nowadays it doesn't work like that so much, so the way I was told was to do things like frequent clubs, meetup societies and internet forums dedicated to the old Northern cultures and world-views. While keeping their affiliation secret they can still make it known subtly, that they have crossed over. If they do that contact will eventually be made.'

That was quite an ear-full coming from a fellow who seldom spoke in long sentences. I nodded at what he had told me and committed it to memory.

'So they make themselves known and a representative of the Brotherhood will contact them?'

'That is one method I've been told about,' he said. 'Don't forget also that some people like to act solely on their own and these solo members don't do a lot of contacting.'

'I see,' I said.

'Another thing is that the Odin Brotherhood sometimes contacts a person once in a lifetime. Sometimes the Odin Brotherhood may make more frequent contacts, maybe through initiated members or actually meeting in person. I have been told of personal, face-to-face meetings; one-on-ones and larger gatherings.'

'That is very interesting,' I said. Crow had covered a bit about this kind of thing before in our talks.

'Another tidbit for you is that even when people do actually meet contacts from the Odin Brotherhood they remain mystical and cryptic. I have heard of such "agents" if you want to use that word, giving people business cards with false information on it, phone numbers that have been disconnected and even addresses that are of occult significance. I don't know much more than that but everything they do has a reason and is usually a teaching of some kind.'

'Wow,' I said. 'I would really like to know more about that.'

He raised his hands slightly in an open handed gesture. 'That's about all I know about it,' he said. 'You already know about contacts made to people who are interested and before they Sojourn. If people already have contact before they cross over then they can let their contacts know that. Then they will probably be contacted.'

I thanked Crow for that.

'Some things I imagine are reserved for people that have crossed the Sojourn line,' I said.

'Yes,' he said. 'I have no doubt of that. But I will tell you something else man: if you venture beyond this point and think about walking the Sojourn you gotta understand that you will be taking a big step into an even bigger world. If you take that step you will become part of something greater than you can imagine. You will become part of history whether you believe it or not.'

A voice on the speakers announced departures for several different busses and advised passengers to go to various gates.

Crow looked up. 'I'm in that batch so I better get a fire lit,' he said.

'Taking the bus and not a train?' I asked.

Crow hoisted his pack onto his shoulder and adjusted it. It looked like it weighed a considerable amount.

'There are no trains going where I am going, bud,' he said. 'Besides, the bus has always been a fun thing for me. You can jump off a bus just about anywhere along the highway. You can't always do that with a train.'

I had done that myself. Most long distance bus drivers were more than happy to let a person off on the side of a road as long as they had sufficient notice. I had used that method to get into one or two hiking trails in the past.

I didn't bother asking Crow where he was going. I knew that my question would be met either by a crafty smile, silence or a change of subject.

We started walking toward a departure gate.

'You know, I have learned a fair bit about you from our talks,' he said. 'I have had a good time in our discussions. I especially liked the camp-out.'

That was an interesting experience. I told him that I too had had a good time during that little adventure.

'Good times,' he said. 'Good memories.'

I agreed with that as well.

'I wish you well on your journey,' I said. 'Watch out for frostbite and bears.'

He chuckled and nodded.

We approached the departure area and I saw that there was a little gate there with a man checking tickets. Beyond him was an open door and a lot in which several large Greyhound-style buses sat idling and boarding passengers. I suspected that I would not be able to pass a certain point without a ticket.

We stood for a moment and finished our coffees in silence.

After that we tossed the cups in a nearby recycling bin and walked the last little bit to where, with one lady ahead of us, the ticket-taker waited.

'Well bud, this is it,' Crow said at last. 'Wish me luck.'

I did and I meant it. I knew what he was going off to do and I was aware of the many dangers that could await a person in the mountains in the dead of winter. I though briefly of Dust-legs' journey and from that I imagined that many strange things were capable of happening in the embrace of raw nature and the Gods.

I reached out my hand and Crow took it. His grip was firm and sure. His grey-green eyes were bright and he had that crafty, trickster grin on his face all over again.

He turned and gave the man his ticket. It was time for him to go through the gate.

He turned toward me one last time before proceeding through and said, 'Keep writing, bud. I hope I see your book in print one day.'

I smiled. 'I hope so too.'

He waved and began to turn to the gate. Other passengers were approaching with their tickets in hand and he did not want to hold up the line.

I stepped out of their way and off to one side of the gate.

'Have a great trip, man,' I said as he began to walk to the first bus. 'We'll see you around.'

Crow suddenly stopped. He turned to look over his shoulder at me, his breath visible now in the frosty December air. I saw that the usual wry grin he usually wore was replaced with an almost forlorn sadness. This seemed reflected in his eyes as well.

'No, brother,' he said. 'You won't.'

Resources for Further Study

Bellows, Henry Adams. *The Poetic Edda: Translated from the Icelandic with an Introduction and Notes*. New York:-American Scandinavian Foundation, 1923.

Hollander, Lee M. *The Poetic Edda: Translated with an Introduction and Explanatory Notes*. Austin: University of Texas Press, 1962.

Larrington, Carolyne. *The Poetic Edda: Translated with an Introduction and Notes*. Oxford: Oxford University Press, 1996.

Mirabello, Mark. *The Odin Brotherhood*. 5th Edition. Oxford: Mandrake of Oxford, 2003.

Teachings of the Odin Brotherhood. Portland: Thule Publications, no date.

Terry, Patricia. *Poems of the Elder Edda*. Philadelphia: University of Pennsylvania Press, 1990.

Thorsson, Edred. *Futhark: A Handbook of Rune Magic*. Boston: Red Wheel/Weiser, 1988.

Storyteller, Ragnar. *Odin's Return*. Payson, Arizona: World Tree Publications, 1995.

Sturluson, Snorri. *Edda*. Trans. Anthony Faulkes. London:-Dent, 1987.

Sturluson, Snorri. *The Prose Edda: Tales from Norse Mythology*. Trans and ed. Jean Young. Berkeley, University of California Press, 1954.

Wodanson, Edred. *The World Tree: An Introduction to the Ancient Ancestral Religion of Asatru*. Union Bay, BC, Canada: Wodanesdag Press, 1995.

- - -. *Asatru – The Hidden Fortress*. Union Bay, BC, Canada: Wodanesdag Press, 1995.

- - -. *A Way of Wyrd*. Union Bay, BC, Canada: Wodanesdag Press, 1997.

The Odin Brotherhood
By Mark L. Mirabello
ISBN 978-1869928-711 £10.99 /$10 paperback / 128pp.

Odinism and the Mysteries of the Past; The Odin Brotherhood
Today and the Heroic Ideal; On Polytheism and the Nature of the
Gods The Eddaic Verses and the Three Ages of Man; Why
Venerate the Odinist Gods? The Contacts between Men and
Gods; The God Odin and His Mysteries; The Goddess Frigg and
the Rite of Marriage ; The God Thor, the Nemesis of Titans; The
Goddess Sif, the Mischief of Loki, and the Skill of the Rock Dwarf;
Heimdall and "The-Sojourn-of-the-Brave"; Bragi, the Holy Words,
and the Seasonal Rites; Idun and Her Enchanted Fruit; Brave Tyr,
the Warrior God; The God Njord, Magic, and the Vanir Gods; The
God Frey and the Elves; Freyja, the Lovely Patroness of Birth; The
God Balder and the Adventure of Death; Nanna and the Odinist
Death Rite; The Legend of "The-Mountain-of-Promise"; Destiny,
Ragnarok, the Mysteries of the Future

Secrets of Asgard
By Ongkowidjojo Vincent
Foreword by David Beth,
Introduction Freya Aswynn
ISBN 978-1-906958-31-2, £12.99/$23 circa 280pp, ills.

In two parts, *Secrets of Asgard* discusses their theoretical and a
practical aspects. Part one focusses centres on the meaning of the
individual runes and the myths, esplaining the Aettir alongside
Northern mythology. It describes each of the gods as well as the
Nine Worlds etc. The second part centres on the application of the
system, namely magic and divinatio and includes rituals and exercises.

A thesis of practical rune magic is developed which is based on the *Havamal* 144 stanza.
The analysis concludes that the Runes were traditionally regarded as actual spirits. The
stanza explains how to make your own set as well as other talismanic objects. The practice
of *galdr*-singing is discussed in more depth to complement the *Havamal* 144 techniques.
Then, a discourse is given on the most common Ancient Germanic magical formulae.
They complement the practical work on talismanic objects.

Visual Magick: - A Manual of Freestyle Shamanism
By Jan Fries ISBN 978-1869928-575 / £10.99/$20/ 196pp

A new edition of the highly acclaimed manual of freestyle shamanism, Suitable for all those inspired by such figures as Austin Spare and Aleister Crowley, and who feel the imperative to develop one's own unique magick way. Visual Magick aims to build vision, imagination, and creative magick. It shows how magicians, witches, artists and therapists can improve visionary abilities, enhance imagination, activate the inner senses, and discover new modes of Trance awareness. The emphasis is on direct experience and the reader is asked to think, act, do, and enjoy as s/he wills.

Seidways Shaking, Swaying & Serpent Mysteries
By Jan Fries ISBN 978-1869928-360/ £12.99/$23/ 350pp

The definitive study of magical trance and possession techniques. The author is inspired by the Nordic tradition of Seidr, said to have been taught to the human race by Odin. The book provides an extensive survey of the manifestation of this powerful technique through several related magical traditions - shamanisn, mesmerism, draconian cults and the nightside of European paganism.

Bright From the Well By Dave Lee
ISBN 978-1869928-841 £10.99/$18 paperback

'Bright From the Well' consists of five stories plus five essays and a rune-poem. The stories revolve around themes from Norse myth - the marriage of Frey and Gerd, the story of how Gullveig-Heidh reveals her powers to the gods, a modern take on the social-origins myth Rig's Tale, Loki attending a pagan pub moot and the Ragnarok seen through the eyes of an ancient shaman. The essays include examination of the Norse creation or origins story, of the magician in or against the world and a chaoist's magical experiences looked at from the standpoint of Northern magic.'

Order direct from
Mandrake of Oxford
PO Box 250, Oxford, OX1 1AP (UK)
Phone: 01865 243671
online at - www.mandrake.uk.net
Email: mandrake@mandrake.uk.net

www.ingramcontent.com/pod-product-compliance
Lightning Source LLC
Chambersburg PA
CBHW020402030726
47496CB00007B/2265